Edgar blinks several time[...] [...] through his head. He ta[...] [...] a smi[...] [...] and then faces forward again, but this time he peers down at his lap. This silence makes me nervous. Maybe I erred in asking him. As I stand to leave, Edgar speaks.

"I used to read her a story every night before she went to sleep. It was about a young girl whose father had a cup of blue stars that he had stored away for her. Whenever the young girl in the story was in trouble at school, had a falling out with a friend or was in pain, her father would reach into his cup of blue stars and give her one. The stars were magical, and they would always have the power to fix the young girl's problems. The night before my Mercedes died, she asked me if I could get her her very own cup of blue stars. She told me, with that cup, I would always be there to help her out." Edgar turns to me with that sad but hopeful face he wore in the mornings. "I need to find a cup of blue stars. It's the only way to get her back, the only way we can be together again."

Of all the explanations Edgar could have given me, I do not expect this one. I close my eyes and choke back a sob. Speechless, all I can do is reach my hand to his and grasp it. Edgar recoils at my touch. He stands with his arms by his side and shouts. "You think I'm crazy! My wife thought so, too! Maybe I am. But the hell with all of you! I know there are blue stars out there, and I'll find them!"

The outburst over, his shoulders sag and his chin dips. Lowering his voice, he adds, "I've got to see if they work."

My eyes grow moist as Edgar shuffles away from the bench.

To: Kova
Thank you so much for
all the love + support!
you are the best!

# BLUE STARS

## AND OTHER TALES OF DARKNESS

## BY TONY TREMBLAY

# ACKNOWLEDGEMENTS

A vigorous nod goes to my wife and family, including future readers Anistyn, Shane, and Anthony (my grandchildren).

An extreme hat tip to Stacey Longo, Rob Smales, Claudia McCoy, Lynne Duhaime, Nancy Kalanta, the Horror World gang, and my Facebook friends.

Huge hugs go to the Blank Page writers group and the Goffstown Library.

Heaps of thanks to all the publishers who initially took the chance on these tales.

A smile big enough for a robin to nest in goes out to my Necon family, those that attended and assisted with NoCon, NEHW members, and all those involved with The Taco Society Presents.

It is my fondest wish to acknowledge Christopher Golden and Connie Golden, the great James A. Moore and Tessa Moore, Tom Deady and Sheila Deady, Scott Goudsward, Bracken MacLeod and Heather MacLeod, John McIlveen and Roberta Colasanti, for all their support and love.

My eternal gratitude to these author friends who pointed me in the right direction by shaping my imagination: Gary Braunbeck, Tom Piccrilli, Linda Addison, and Gerard Houarner.

This book would not be possible without the efforts of David Dodd, David Wilson, and Trish Wilson. Thank you so much.

Tom Deady receives a second acknowledgement for generously agreeing to write the forward to this book. I'm honored beyond words.

Finally, my warmest regards goes out to you, dear readers. Thank you.

# DEDICATION

This book is dedicated to Sandi Bixler and Robert Perreault.

# TABLE OF CONTENTS

# INTRODUCTION

## TONY TREMBLAY: THE PERSON BEHIND THE WORDS

Like many writers of speculative fiction and horror, Tony Tremblay is a paradox. Tony Tremblay, the writer, pens stories that are dark and menacing, often violent and heartbreaking. Yet Tony Tremblay, the person, is one of the warmest and kindest men you'll ever meet. He is a great conversationalist, knowledgeable on so many topics. He is funny and cheerful and always has a smile and a kind word for you. So, which is the *real* Tony?

Before you turn the page and begin reading Tony Tremblay's stories, there are a few things you need to know about him—because after you finish his stories, you won't believe a word I've written about him. First, Tony is a devoted family man and a loyal, caring friend. He enjoys a good scotch and an occasional cigar, and he's a fiercely proud resident of Goffstown, New Hampshire—you'll often see him wearing a cap bearing his hometown's name. I was a fan of Tony Tremblay, the *person*, long before I became a fan of his writing. A lot of who Tony is seeps into his stories. Now, about those stories...

I became a fan of Tony Tremblay, the *writer*, after reading "Blue Stars" in the Necon anthology *Now I Lay Me Down to Sleep*. It's a devastating story of loss, heartbreak, and kindness gone wrong. It's one of those stories that will stay with you long after you put it down. Then, just when you think it has faded like the fragile memory of a dream, you see a person sitting alone in a restaurant or at the park, and it all comes rushing back and breaks you again. That's the clout Tony Tremblay's writing holds. "Blue Stars" is included in the very book you are holding: you've been warned.

Let's talk more about this book. "Blue Stars" is just one example of Tony's talent. His writing takes on so many shapes that it's impossible to define it in any single genre. "Steel" is a post-apocalyptic story of survival, but the very next story, "The Scum Bar", is a gritty noir tale of betrayal. "The Thaumaturge" is historical fantasy/horror, followed by "Eyes" which is…what? Weird, bizarro fiction? "Incident on N.H. Route 666" and "The Reverend's Wife" are two stories I won't even *try* to put a label on. After you read them, you'll know what I mean. And so, it goes. Thirteen stories in all, each unique and powerful.

There *is* something that ties all of Tony's stories together—his ability to mesmerize the reader with his words. Tony uses words first to seduce you, to lull you and welcome you into his world. Then he turns those words into weapons, sharp objects and blunt instruments to cut you with and bludgeon you. To leave you spent and breathless. And, those words leave scars and nightmares in their wake. But they'll also leave you wanting more, because that is the nature and power of beautiful writing.

The time has come for us to part ways, and for you to journey into the many worlds of Tony Tremblay. I recommend a well-lit room and perhaps a box of tissues for the trip. You might hit a few rough spots on the ride, but when you come out on the other side, you'll have had the pleasure of meeting Tony Tremblay, the writer. The only thing better is to meet Tony Tremblay, the person.

Tom Deady
December 2018

*Tom Deady's first novel, HAVEN, won the 2016 Bram Stoker Award for Superior Achievement in a First Novel. Tom's second novel, ETERNAL DARKNESS, was released in early 2017. His other works include WEEKEND GETAWAY and BACKWATER.*

# STORY NOTES (STEEL)

*A* voice popped into my head one evening as I was drifting off to sleep. The voice was male, young, deadpan. It spoke, "We all watched Frankie die." The phrase was loud, clear, and it jolted me awake. I jumped out of bed and wrote the sentence down.

I thought about that prompt for over a month. My one-way commute to work is ninety minutes, and in that time, I was able to concoct a short story around the phrase. It led me to an apocalyptic tale, which I submitted to a writers-exercise group in the old Horror World website. That story, "Burning Rain", is the last tale in this collection.

Months after I wrote the story, I started work on a novella titled The Sad Saga of Mattie Dyer (The Seeds of Nightmares, published by Crossroad Press). When Mattie was finished, I thought about expanding it into a novel, and with some tinkering, "Burning Rain" would have been a good fit. Time wasn't on my side however, as the deadline for Seeds was creeping up so I put the project aside.

The Seeds of Nightmares was released in January 2017, and the following July, I attended a wedding of two good friends. Also at the wedding was Stacey Longo, an author and publisher whom I had met a few years earlier at a convention called Necon.

Whenever you get a group of authors together, you can expect talk about writing, some gossip, and future projects. This wedding was no exception. Stacey, myself, and another author, Kristi Petersen Schoonover, were standing by a tree with drinks in our hands, when I put forth a suggestion. "How about the three of us each write a novella and find someone to publish it?" Alcohol consumption may have played a part in the over-enthusiastic response, but it was agreed by

*all that it was a wonderful idea, and Stacey offered to publish the book.*
*This was my chance to expand "Burning Rain" into a novella.*

*Using the premise of "Burning Rain", I began work on* Steel. *I wanted it to be fast-paced—almost all non-stop action. The apocalyptic theme remained, with a reluctant, strong female lead propelling the narrative. I wanted the story to be bleak—soul-crunchingly bleak.*

*When finished, I submitted* Steel *to Stacey, and she proclaimed it worthy of publication.* Steel *appeared in* Triplicity: The Terror Project Volume One *(Books and Boos Press) alongside excellent novellas by Stacey, and Rob Smales. (Kristi's novella would appear in volume two).*

*While* Steel *is not a sequel to* The Sad Saga of Mattie Dyer, *they do share plot threads—primarily, my fascination with holes. Stumbling upon a hole is an aberration; it always leads to no good. My advice is to avoid them at all costs.*

# STEEL

## CHAPTER ONE

The voice beside her was choked, high-pitched and pleading.

"Please! Save her! Save Mel!"

There wasn't anything Steel could do. There was nothing *any* of them could do. They stood at the windows, looked between the bars, and watched Melancholy die.

Though Steel couldn't hear much of anything outside their shelter's walls, she knew Melancholy's skin was sizzling, making popping noises as the burning rain pelted her. It was the kind of noise a damp log makes when thrown onto a fire.

They all looked on in agonized silence as Melancholy's hair ignited. Puffs of steam floated above her head, but it didn't rise very high before the rain, and what little breeze there was smothered it.

Steel was glad Melancholy wasn't close to the windows; the odor would have been awful. One of the worst smells is human hair when it's burning, though it fascinated Steel to watch it curl up when touched by a flame. The pain Melancholy felt had to be tremendous, though she never screamed, not even once.

The burning rain beat down harder and Melancholy melted, as if she were made of wax. Her forehead drooped, her flesh turning into a slow-moving wave of pink sludge. Her eyes widened and bulged to the point of bursting. In an instant, they disappeared, flushed away in a tide of lava-like skin. Steel and the other spectators leaned toward the window, battling an urge to turn and pull away from the sight. But, every one of them continued to look on, grimacing as Melancholy's nose wilted and dripped down onto her lips. The skin on Melancholy's face had turned into a ball of misshapen flesh. It clung to her chin, deciding where to go next. Finally, like taffy stretching, it slipped, pooling and forming a gooey mass on her breasts.

As still as a statue, Melancholy continued melting. The rain ate its way through her clothes and skin, working its way through her muscles. Her insides squeezed through newly formed cavities and dribbled to the ground. The organs liquefied after contact with the rain, landing at her feet, forming chunky puddles. Like stew left too long in a cooking pot, they boiled away until they were blackened. Her skeleton remained upright, until the rain pitting her bones made them so fragile they cracked under their own weight. They split off in brittle pieces, fell to the ground and joined the chunky stock of Melancholy's remains.

It was something a sane person never got used to.

The hardest part would be cleaning up the remains the next morning after the burning rains had stopped: there was nothing worse than stepping in that shit.

They all turned from the windows and slunk back to the main area. There was plenty of room for them to sit as their numbers had dwindled to half their original total in the last few months. Melancholy might have been the latest of their group to die, but she wouldn't be the last.

Melancholy was the second to end her own life.

Taking a seat in one of the rocking chairs they had salvaged from a nearby apartment, Steel hung her head. The rocker was missing its left armrest; her arm hung limp at her side.

"Do you think she did it on purpose?"

It was the voice that had pleaded at the window. It belonged to nine-year-old Daisy, the youngest of their group. Steel glanced up at the girl, looked into her teary black eyes, and held her gaze for a moment. It was a stalling tactic—she needed a few seconds to figure out how to answer the question.

The burning rain started at the same time each evening, and everyone knew they had to be inside the shelter before the rust-colored clouds reached them. The clouds arrived slowly: enough warning to seek refuge in the shelter. Even the few remaining animals knew enough to take cover when the daylight began to tint red. For some unknown reason, Melancholy had ignored the clouds this evening.

Melancholy had sat about twenty feet in front of the shelter on a car seat pulled from an old Ford when the clouds had crested the city's skyline. When the rest of their group had run past, telling her to get her ass in gear, she had refused to move. She'd been reading one of the books that Wise had placed in their bookcase. Steel had no choice but to close and bolt the door.

They had all rushed to the windows and watched what had taken place.

A raindrop had landed on Melancholy's hand, causing the book to fall to the ground, splayed open. She had stared at the book for a full minute before she had moved. Finally, she'd stood, turned, and faced the shelter. Her gaze had gone directly to the windows.

Maybe Melancholy had wanted one last look at them. Had it been her way of saying goodbye? Had her blank expression been an accusation of some kind? Steel wasn't sure what her intentions had been. Seconds later, when the clouds burst and the burning rain fell in earnest, the look on Melancholy's face never wavered. There was no doubt in Steel's mind the girl had wanted to die.

At the time Steel had thought, *what a waste*.

"No, Daisy, I don't think Mel did it on purpose," Steel finally replied. "I'm guessing that she fell asleep while reading and didn't wake up in time. When she did wake up, she was groggy and it was too late to save herself."

The tears flowed heavily from Daisy's eyes. She turned her head so Steel wouldn't see her sobbing then shuffled over to her sleeping area where she curled into a ball with her back to Steel. Daisy hadn't reached out to her for comfort, and Steel hadn't expected her to. Daisy might have been only nine years old, but she took easy to the ways of the world. Shit happens all the time. Daisy had to deal with it in her own way and then move on.

Steel tore her eyes away from Daisy and glanced around the room. As expected, the other six surviving members of the group were staring at her. Their question for her would be different from Daisy's. She could tell what they were thinking by looking into their eyes.

*Why?*

"I don't know why Mel didn't come in from the burning rain," Steel began. "But if this was planned, she didn't tell me or hint that she was going to stay out there this evening. I'm hoping that it was an accident—that she fell asleep or lost track of the time."

"Bullshit!"

Steel didn't have to look in his direction to know who voiced the angry disclaimer. Rock was always the one challenging her, questioning her decisions, trying to take leadership of the group away from her. She turned to him. "You got something to say, then say it."

"Mel wanted to die!" Rock's retort was loud and venomous. "She was tired and hungry. She couldn't take it anymore." Spittle flew from his lips. "She hated staying in this damned shelter and wasting away!"

Steel sighed. It always came down to this. Rock wanted to leave the shelter and take to the land outside the city. He believed there were others out there like them, in larger numbers, who managed to make surviving easier. But, Steel knew there was another reason: Rock was sixteen, the oldest of the boys, and she couldn't help but notice his constant erections. Steel had slept with him in the past as a way to relieve her boredom. His oversized ego and possessive tendencies put a stop to it, and she had no intention of doing so again.

"Look," she began, "we're tired and we're hungry. And—"

A crash against the north wall, thunderous enough to penetrate its thickness, caused them all to jerk their heads. A second later, the ground lurched. Screams pierced Steel's ears as everyone stumbled to find a handhold. A second crash came, then another. Piles of clothing avalanched off beds, cookware rattled in the sink, and wall hangings tumbled from their anchors. The shelter continued to shake violently, with only short pauses between the attacks. Repeated collisions took their toll on the other three walls. They weakened, and their shaking grew stronger with every impact. A large, lit kerosene lantern sitting on a makeshift table skipped along with every crash until it slipped off the surface. Greasy shards of yellowed glass littered the floor, and a newly split seam at the base released its contents. Some of the kerosene splashed low onto a concrete wall, but most of it spread along the floor following a path of least resistance. Flames chased the fuel.

Months of training kicked in. Some of them rushed to smother the flame with blankets while others built a dam around the flowing liquid with sandbags. The battering at the north wall remained constant, adding to the confusion and fear of the fire. Hearing a cry, Steel turned to its source.

"Put it out! Put it out!"

It was Fleet, running in circles, his arm on fire.

Steel ran to Fleet and tackled him to the floor. She flipped him over on his stomach, and hoped to extinguish the flame by lying on his arm. He wiggled trying to slide out from beneath her in his panic, but Steel had a weight and muscle advantage over him. Feeling the heat of the flames through her clothes, she pushed down harder trying to smother the fire. She raised her head and attempted a quick assessment of her surroundings to see if anyone else was in trouble. But, with smoke and concrete dust swirling around in the air, she couldn't see more than a couple of feet. From what she could view, and from the snatches of conversation she could hear, it looked as though the others had managed not only to contain the fire but to put it out.

She also caught a glimpse of Rock standing rigid, cowering against the front door, his eyes wide with terror.

*Leader, my ass.*

The building stopped shaking and, thankfully, Fleet stopped struggling beneath her. Telling him to lie still, she rose and then inspected the damage to his arm. He was lucky for two reasons. First off, while his arm was going to sting like hell for the next few days, his burns didn't appear to be very bad. Only a small amount of kerosene had splashed on him and it hadn't soaked into his clothes. Secondly, the oil had missed his legs. Fleet was the fastest runner they had; they'd be screwed if he were out of action for any length of time.

Fleet looked into Steel's eyes. She couldn't miss the gratitude in them.

"Go and put some salve on that arm, Fleet, and wrap a bandage around it. All we have is aspirin, but it should help with the pain." Fleet nodded, lifted himself from the floor, and made his way to the first aid kit.

"Was it a basher?"

Steel turned to see Cookie staring at her. Cookie's full frame shook, and her mouth twitched nervously. With all that had happened to them since the burning rains had first come, Steel marveled that Cookie was as plump as ever. Though food was scarce and they rationed what they could scavenge, Cookie's body somehow managed to hold onto every scrap of food she ate. She was only fourteen, but she was twice as thick as any two of them, and her breasts hung heavy on her chest.

*Another reason why Rock seems to have a perpetual erection.*

Steel gazed around their shelter and answered Cookie. "Yeah, more than likely. But, everything seems to be okay. Those concrete walls are eight inches thick. They ain't getting in here."

"You sure?"

Steel looked deep into Cookie's eyes. "I'm sure."

Cookie nodded back in relief.

"Now go and help the others clean up. I'm going to take a walk around and see if the basher caused any damage."

Bashers hunted in the evening, never this early. Steel and the others secured themselves in the shelter every night. If this *was* the work of a basher, it would be one more problem they didn't need. Bashers were the only animals immune to the burning rain, but that didn't make them the most dangerous. Other animals, the ones that hunted during daylight, were the ones they feared more. Still, you couldn't take bashers lightly.

Once, Steel and Rock had found a dead one while hunting for food. They had cut up the carcass and brought it back to the shelter in several trips. Her stomach growled at the memory—that basher had fed them all for weeks. They were ugly brutes with their square heads and all, as big as some of those rusted cars that lined the streets in the city. Their eyes, nose, mouth, and ears were recessed, tucked away safely inside their battering-ram-like skulls. Bashers also had an acute sense of hearing, which was how they detected prey. With that thought, Steel swore silently to herself. The basher that attacked the shelter must have heard Rock's shouting earlier. She was all set to go have it out with him when something on the west wall caught her attention. She froze, focusing.

Steel walked casually over to the wall. Although she did not want to cause alarm, she couldn't help herself: she gasped. There was a thin crack, about two feet long, running from the floor and up the wall. As her eyes followed the crevice, she knew at once that it was not a spider's web or a stain. Closing her eyes, she rocked back slightly on her heels and held her breath—if only she could will it away. When a hand clamped onto her shoulder, she jumped.

"How bad is it?"

She recognized the voice and her tension drained. It was Stealth. He was a year younger than Rock, but, when it came to maturity, Stealth was without a doubt, Rock's senior. She kept her back to him and answered without taking her eyes off the crack.

"It's not too bad. The shelter's not going to collapse or anything. But, it's not good. I don't think it'll spread on its own, though that wall's not gonna hold if a basher keeps at it. We're gonna have to patch it up and hope that it's enough."

"Well," Stealth said, "we know they hunt alone and they ain't all that smart, so it's not likely they'll notice it and decide to bash away at it. Maybe tomorrow we can put something in front of it, you know, outside, so they can't get to it."

Steel finally turned and faced him. "Yeah, that's a good idea. No sense worrying everyone tonight. Let's tell them in the morning. We might be able to roll one of those old cars over. That should keep them away from the wall."

"You're looking tired, Steel. How about heading to bed?"

Steel sighed. "Yeah, that sounds like a good idea."

"I've got room, if you care to join me."

The offer wasn't entirely unexpected. She'd slept with Stealth before, too. She'd slept with all the older boys and had come to realize it wasn't a good idea. Most of those she had slept with were dead now—one of them by her own hand. She wasn't going to make the same mistake again.

"No," she said quietly, "I'm going to sleep by myself." Steel could read the disappointment in his eyes. "I'm going to make sure the shelter is cleaned up from the fire and I'll check on Daisy. Then, I'm heading to bed—my own bed. I suggest you do the same. It's been two days without any real food and we're going to have to go deep into the city tomorrow, which means waking up early. Get some sleep."

Stealth headed toward his bed while Steel did a lap around the shelter, making sure the blankets they had used to kill the fire weren't smoldering and that the kerosene on the floor was cleaned up. As she checked the latches and locks on each of the windows and the front door, her mind wandered. She compared Stealth to Rock, examining their temperament, their leadership abilities, and their intelligence. If the worst happened to her, which one would take her place? She reached her bed without coming to a solid conclusion. Stretched out on her mattress, she decided not to remove her clothes. After turning off the small lantern by her bedside, she lay back and stared at the shadows on the ceiling.

Her last thought before sleep was how she wished that Rock's balls were as big as Stealth's.

# CHAPTER TWO

Whisper woke at sunrise and roused the others from their beds—her job since becoming a member of the group. In her time at the shelter, Whisper had performed her duties efficiently, without the use of verbal prodding. Her lack of speech took some getting used to but now everyone accepted it without question. The only person who had ever heard her speak was Steel, who wasn't sure what she had heard uttered from the young girl's mouth was even a word.

Steel had found Whisper a couple of weeks earlier on one of their rare foraging missions away from the city. They were in a remote wooded area that Wise, for some unknown reason, had always cautioned them not to enter. But, they had been desperate for food at the time and had no qualms about going in. Besides, Wise was dead, and there was no one to stop them.

From outward appearances, the house hadn't been vandalized, so Steel had been cautiously optimistic about their chances of finding something to eat. Her hopes had been dashed when she circled around the house and discovered the back door wide open. Once inside, she heard sounds coming from the upper level. With her right hand, she had reached down and gripped the handle of the weapon fastened to her left hip. With a tight hold on it, she had crept up a carpeted staircase to investigate.

The sounds had been coming from a room at the end of the hallway.

Steel had trodden lightly past a bathroom and a child's bedroom, and then tiptoed to the doorway at the end of the hall and had peered into the room. Against a far corner of the wall, two males had a young girl cornered. The men were naked, and while Steel's view was limited to their backs, it was obvious what they had in mind. The girl had been cowering and whimpering; her eyes, wide with fear, were directed below the men's waists.

Steel had slowly unsheathed her katana, a weapon she carried on foraging missions. The extra care she had taken to sharpen the sword the night before proved to have been a prudent use of her time, the blade so well-honed she'd had no doubt as to how effective it would be. It had taken only two swings to lop off their heads.

The young girl had screamed as the bodies had collapsed to the floor, then quieted when she glared at her own outstretched hands. The men's blood had speckled them red. The girl's intermittent sobs had echoed off the walls.

When the girl had calmed down, she looked up, directly into Steel's eyes, and whispered one word:

"Thanks."

Over the ensuing days, Steel wondered if Whisper had even spoken. Perhaps she had only mouthed the word, and Steel herself had put the voice to it.

Steel and the girl had dragged the bodies outdoors to where the rest of the foraging party had waited. Whisper had returned with Steel and their bounty to the shelter, but the girl had refused to engage in any conversation during the journey. Throughout the day, none of them had been able to get much information out of the girl, who insisted on communicating only with her hands. They did manage to learn that she was sixteen years old, still a long way from becoming an adult. They welcomed her as the newest member of their group, and Steel gave her the name Whisper.

Steel now felt Whisper's hand on her shoulder, gently shaking her awake.

When Steel opened her eyes, the young girl was leaning over and smiling. Steel had been taken with Whisper's innocent countenance and her beauty since that day she had found her in the house. For the first time in what seemed like ages, Steel found herself smiling.

Steel planted her feet firmly on the floor and lifted both

arms to stretch the kinks out of her back. When she turned to speak to Whisper, she saw the girl had disappeared. A portion of Steel, larger than she cared to admit, was disappointed with Whisper's absence.

Steel's empty belly rumbled but she made a determined effort to ignore it by concentrating on her surroundings. Around the shelter, everyone else was already up, preparing for a trip into the city. Reluctantly, she shuffled to a small alcove at the south wall. The middle of the alcove contained a built-in storage area flush to the floor. She dropped to her knees, lifted the lid, and removed a container of liquid that was much too large for its meager contents. She raised it to her mouth, using both hands, and drank, careful not to let any of it spill from her lips. A basher had an extraordinary sense of smell—blood-stained clothing was just as effective as a shout that there was fresh prey nearby. After taking two small sips, she replaced the container, closed the lid and walked back to her sleeping area.

Steel removed her katana from its peg on her headboard and fastened it onto her hip. Wise had given her the weapon shortly after he had introduced her to the group. More importantly, he had taught her how to use it. She had been a fast learner. She stood by her bed and waited for the prompt. It took only a few more minutes for everyone to get their gear and weapons at the ready, and then they all stood at attention by their own beds. One at a time, they nodded at her. She nodded back and then led them out of the shelter.

Once outside, Steel informed them about the crack on the west wall. There were murmurs and a few exchanged glances with wide eyes. Steel walked over to the crack. They all followed her and inspected it together. Though she noticed the nervousness on their faces, none of them replied with much more than a grunt or a sigh. She recounted her conversation with Stealth after they had discovered the crack. Afterward, she announced their first order of business was to find an automobile with four good tires. She assigned Stealth, Rock, Fleet, and Whisper to the task. Next, she asked Cookie to clean up Melancholy's remains. Steel then called Daisy to her side and told everyone that she and Daisy were going to look through the maps to plan that days foraging expedition. When no one spoke up, Steel nodded to the group. They all nodded in return and went off to their assigned tasks.

# CHAPTER THREE

Fleet, Stealth, Rock, and Whisper, paraded down the main road, single file, away from the shelter and toward the city. Fleet knew they wouldn't have to travel far to find an abandoned car—there were plenty lined up along the road outside the shelter. Finding one with four good tires and a key in the ignition to unlock the steering wheel would prove tricky, though. Since the terrain was level, pushing it wouldn't be too strenuous. With Whisper steering, there would be enough strength among the three boys to overcome any slight inclines.

Without discussion, Rock assumed control of the mission, which irritated Fleet, though he reined in his objections. Rock, after all, was the oldest of the group, though not necessarily the smartest or bravest. Fleet had seen Rock cowering by the door the previous evening during the fire, but decided this was not the time to bring it up. Rock had a tendency to be ill-tempered, or hot-headed as Wise had once more accurately described it. Because Rock had the only working firearm in the group, Fleet thought it best to wait until the evening when all weapons would be stored before he confronted Rock over leadership during a mission.

Everyone carried a weapon except for Whisper. She steadfastly refused when one was offered. Stealth and Fleet both carried long knives they'd taken from a pawnshop almost a year ago—not long after the world had turned to shit and all the adults had gone crazy. The long knives had saved both their asses in the past, but if Fleet had his druthers, he would have been more than happy to carry a firearm. A few months ago, Rock had found the rifle and a stockpile of ammo in the basement of one of the houses they'd foraged. He claimed it for himself, and Steel hadn't objected, so the rifle remained in his possession. They figured that the remaining ones had been taken by the still-sane and desperate before they, too, had changed.

Though Rock assumed the leadership of the group, Fleet made the decision on his own to take point. It was not unusual— he often led the way on their foraging missions. His curiosity had always been strong, enough so to tamp down any fear gene he might have been born with. He was always the first to enter a building or, to the consternation of the others of the group, stick his head into places that the others dared not. He was not only fearless, but fast as hell. Wise had chosen his name, and it fit perfectly.

Fleet was the only one of the group who could outrun a gorildog, and they used his talent more than a few times when they had been desperate for food. Fleet would purposely show himself to a gorildog, then lead the animal into an ambush, usually a dead-end street where the rest of their group lay in wait. For Fleet's safety, they always ensured a way out of the ambush, such as an open window to jump through or a dumpster to hop into in case their attempt to kill the animal failed. So far, Fleet was three for three without any close calls.

The four of them trudged down the road, each making soundless judgments on the worthiness of the automobiles they passed. It was obvious which ones couldn't be moved. A quarter mile from the shelter, Fleet spied one that might do the job. It was small enough to be pushed without much effort but large enough to cover the crack in the wall. More importantly, none of its tires looked flat.

Fleet whistled softly and pointed. As he trotted over to the vehicle to inspect it, Rock and Stealth rushed to join him. They kicked the tires and looked inside to see if there was a key in the ignition. Stealth noted that there was a keychain with an attached bottle opener dangling behind the steering wheel. He opened the door and slid into the front seat, mumbled something that sounded like "All right!" to Fleet, then twisted the key. None of them were disappointed when the starter didn't crank; they hadn't expected it to. But, when the steering wheel turned, muted cheering followed. Stealth got out and pushed with the other two to make sure the vehicle was mobile. It was, and Rock declared it would suit their needs.

Facing the vehicle, Rock lifted his arm and signaled for Whisper to join them. Fleet and Stealth turned in her direction to encourage her to come over, but they both stopped short.

Fleet, his brow creased, gazed at Stealth, then both turned to Rock. Confused by their look, Rock's face tightened and tilted to the side. Fleet raised his eyes and shrugged his shoulders. All three turned to look back at the road they had been traveling.

Whisper had vanished.

They swept the area with their eyes.

Rock sighed. Before Fleet could determine if it was out of fear or annoyance, Rock put both of his hands to his mouth and shouted, "WHISPER!"

Fleet's eyes went wide. He couldn't believe what Rock had just done. "Are you crazy? Keep your voice down! We don't want..."

All of their heads turned to the sound of heavy footfalls. The pattern suggested a single animal that sounded close—too close. Fleet wasn't sure what was headed their way. More than likely than it was a gorildog, though from the noise it could be a basher. "Get in the car," he shouted. "Close the doors and lie low."

Rock hesitated. Fleet thought that maybe Rock was angry at being told what to do. With the animal closing in and the danger real, Rock must have swallowed his pride; he followed them into the car. Rock jumped into the front seat while Fleet and Stealth dove into the rear. The seats in the back had been folded down to create a bigger cargo area, but the two of them were still packed in tight.

On their backs, they waited.

Though the doors were shut, and the closed windows muffled the exterior noise, Fleet could hear the animal's approach. Like a stampede of cattle, the sound grew louder until it came to a halt alongside their hiding place. He thought it was alone— he could hear its anger and confusion as it circled the vehicle.

The animal bumped up against the car and snorted. The squeak of its claws digging at metal made him shiver. A refrain went through his head—*I will not look up, I will not look up, I will not look up*—

His face buried to the floor, Fleet waited for the beast to move on.

Everything went quiet.

Fleet remained tense. He held his breath for as long as possible, then let it out through his nostrils with a suppressed hiss. Sweat pouring from his face, he battled imaginary itches as he lay on the folded seats. The burns on his arm had not bothered him since morning, but it now felt as if his skin were on fire again. It took all of his will power not to rub out the stinging. He continued to wait and listen, but the only sound he could hear was everyone's breathing. Time dragged on.

Rock whispered, "I think it's gone."

Stealth nodded in agreement.

Fleet wasn't so sure. "Let's wait a few more minutes, make sure it's safe."

They all nodded and stayed put.

After what felt like an hour to Fleet, Stealth spoke softly. "I'm going to check."

Fleet turned his head to watch.

Stealth shifted his weight onto his elbows and knees. After a muffled grunt, he pushed himself a few inches up from the seats. When finished, he froze.

Fleet tensed. Had Stealth heard something? Was he waiting for a reaction? Or was he too terrified to move? Then, Fleet heard Stealth counting under his breath:

"One—two—" On the count of three, Fleet watched Stealth's head lift. When Stealth's eyes had reached a height where he could see out the window, Fleet held his breath.

Nobody moved inside the automobile, and nothing moved outside of it. Fleet listened. All was quiet.

Stealth's scream broke the silence.

Fleet jerked like a startled dog. He buried his face into the folded seat and brought his hands up to cover his head. He heard a crash, and then felt a tickling sensation all over his back and legs, as if hundreds of spiders were crawling over him.

*I'm going to die.*

Fleet gathered his courage and forced himself into a sitting position. When he saw the cause of Stealth's fright, the volume of his own scream matched that of his friend. A gorildog stood on the other side of the window. Its snout protruded inside the automobile through a hole in the glass. The beast's jaws were closed, the hole too small to allow it to open its mouth. The gorildog's eyes were red, steely, and focused on Stealth.

Fleet realized that while Stealth had had the time to scream, he had little time for anything else.

A massive paw, set with curved and pointed claws, slammed into the window. The glass imploded; hundreds of shards rained over the two of them. The gorildog's paw thrust through the opening and found its target—Stealth's face. Stealth's head flew backward, his body sailing past Fleet into the opposite window, cracking the glass in a web. Stealth's body crumpled to the folded seats, his head trailing a thick red streak on the window. He came to rest against Fleet.

"Aaaaaah!" Fleet cried, trying to push Stealth off his legs. Rock poked his head up from the front seat and wailed at the sight of Stealth's body.

The gorildog reacted to Rock's cries. Like a cat that had cornered a mouse, the beast swung its arm back and forth inside the automobile, searching for its prey. As Fleet leaned back from the beast, its fully extended claws made a grab at him. Despite the threat, Fleet managed to keep himself in control. "Rock," he shouted, "get out of the car and shoot the damn thing!"

After an eternity, Fleet heard the sound of straining door hinges. His head swung to the front door, but his view was limited as he continued to dodge the beast's claws. The gorildog had forced more of its body through the hole—its swipes only inches away from taking Fleet's face off.

*What the hell is Rock waiting for?* He hoped that Rock hadn't run away and left him.

All thoughts of Rock vanished when the gorildog planted his talons into Stealth's neck. A muffled gurgle escaped Stealth's mouth as red bubbles formed between his lips. Blood spurted from the wound, some of it finding its way into Fleet's eyes and mouth. He gagged at the taste.

The gorildog pulled Stealth toward the broken window. Fleet bent forward and wrapped his arms around Stealth's waist. He pulled with all his might, but he was no match for the gorildog's strength.

Fleet extended his legs and tried to jam his feet against the door's wall for leverage. It didn't work. With a violent tug, the gorildog yanked Stealth partway through the window.

Fleet had no choice. He let go of Stealth and fell back to the folded seats.

Prize in hand, the gorildog took a moment to balance itself. It bent forward, then adjusted its grip on Stealth, maneuvering its massive paws until they were wrapped around Stealth's head. The gorildog snarled, sounding as ugly as it looked, exposing rows of stained and broken teeth. It leaned forward and clamped its jaws over Stealth's head. With one quick shake, the beast severed Stealth's head from his torso. What was left of Stealth tumbled out of the car and onto the ground.

Fleet couldn't take his eyes off the gorildog. He watched, heart thumping as fast as it ever had, as the gorildog snapped his jaws shut. Brain matter oozed from between the beast's teeth. It chewed for less than a minute before it swallowed Stealth's whole skull.

The gorildog paused and its head bobbed: first to Fleet, then to the ground, and then back up again.

*Oh my god, it's deciding whether to go after me or to eat what's left of Stealth!*

Though he was ashamed to admit it, Fleet hoped that the beast would pick up the rest of its meal and take off.

The gorildog didn't waste time making up its mind. With arms outstretched and claws extended, the beast released a low-pitched howl, opened its jaws wide, and moved toward the window again. Fleet shuffled backward until his back slammed against the wall of the car. He froze, and stared at the gorildog through the window. The beast's teeth were spotted red, splintered bone and tufts of hair lodged between them. Drool dripped from its bottom jaw. The beast's head turned left, and then right.

*He's studying the interior of the car!*
Its eyes met Fleet's.

When the beast's head exploded, Fleet jumped so high he hit the rooftop. An echo of a gunshot rang in Fleet's ears.

The beast remained standing for a few seconds, and then slipped below Fleet's sight, hitting the ground with a soft thud. As the tension in Fleet's body dissolved, he collapsed onto the folded seats. Rock had come through.

Fleet was emotionally torn between the terror he had just gone through and the gratitude of having survived it. He wanted to cry, but he refused to let Rock see him bawling like a baby. He composed himself just in time—Rock was standing at the broken window. Fleet took comfort in the fact that Rock looked as shaken as he himself felt.

"Come on, get out of there," Rock told him nervously. "That gunshot is sure to bring more of them."

Fleet didn't need to be told twice. He quickly got out of the wrecked car and hurried to Rock's side. In other circumstances they would have brought Stealth's body back with them, or even the gorildog's, but Fleet knew the weight of the bodies would have slowed them down, making them easy pickings. The two of them headed back to the shelter, running hard and not looking back.

When she heard the gunshot, Steel gathered what remained of the group and herded them to the safety of the shelter. An adult couldn't have fired the gun unless he was early in the process of turning, and very few of the young people she had met passing by the shelter had firearms. The sound had been so close it *had* to be Rock, but still, she had taken no chances.

The sounds of banging fists against the door and familiar cries to open it relaxed her some, but her relief had been brief. After Rock and Fleet were let in and she saw that Stealth and Whisper were not among them, Steel had hung her head and let her mind go blank.

As Fleet and Rock recounted their misadventure for the group, grief overwhelmed her. Soon, their words faded into the background.

Steel exhaled softly. As the breath left her lungs and traveled through her lips, a name floated between them. She spoke it quietly, like a whisper, and then it was gone. As she listened to the boys briefing, all confidence in her own leadership turned to depression and self-doubt. She wanted nothing more at this moment than to lie down and go to sleep, and then, with any luck, never wake up.

Steel turned and headed for her bed. Fleet and Rock stopped their report in mid-sentence. She was aware they were watching her, but was too overwhelmed with grief and self-pity to care. Daisy called her name but Fleet quickly shushed her. "Let's give her a moment," he said, placing a hand on Daisy's shoulder. Though his statement was directed to Daisy, they all understood. They turned away to give Steel her privacy.

Steel lay on her bed and stared at the ceiling. *How had it come to this?* Day after day they battled monsters, dodged the burning rain, and scavenged for food... and it was *she* who had to hold the group together. She cursed Wise for putting her in charge when he had, and then she cursed him again, damning him to hell for having died the way he did.

The world had turned crazy about a month before she had met Wise. She recalled the feelings of awe and confusion when the deep red clouds had amassed over part of the city. The thought had never occurred to her that it signaled the end of the world.

Her memory of that first cloud, ruby-colored, perfectly round and dense, appearing out of nowhere and hovering over the U.S. Army's record storage facility, was still sharp. Like a snapshot, the cloud had remained motionless for hours. Crowds had gathered to gawk while the local news stations rushed to cover the story. Rumors had been rife due to its location and strange color. People thought it curious that the wind hadn't dissipated or pushed the cloud along with the currents. Curiosity dissolved into fear when the cloud grew larger and blanketed the city. According to the news reports, it had continued to expand, and in a matter of weeks, it had covered the globe. The rain fell shortly after—not the burning rain that now came every evening, but a slick oily gray rain that had smelled foul and clung to the skin. There was no escaping the gray rain. It seemed to have a life of its own, often finding its way into buildings, and managing, somehow, to reach everybody inside. Everyone it touched had gone insane.

Except for the young people.

The adults had changed immediately after contact with the gray rain. Their cognitive skills declined and their social behaviors regressed. They turned instinctual. Beastly. Hunting meat came naturally to them. Survival, their only priority. After the adults had feasted on their children, they took to the streets. A pack mentality had developed—they formed gangs, and had attacked the young wherever they could find them.

Young people became adept at evading the adults. They had formed small pockets of their own, believing there was safety in numbers. If you judged success by avoiding starvation, hiding from the adults and evading the animals, then the tactic was reliable, though not perfect. Time was still short for those who had not been transformed by the gray rain. No one knew when it would be their time to turn.

Steel had seen it happen twice.

The change came with little warning as the turning age was different for everyone. Steel thought it was connected to an internal clock that they all possessed. Once your body hit that preprogrammed moment, you turned. Everyone she had met who survived both types of rain and the dangers that followed had made it at least to the age of twenty. She refused any survivor into the shelter who admitted to being over nineteen years old.

The gray rain's effect on animals had been just as deadly. Canines grew exceptionally large. Their muscles developed so fast that eventually they could stand on their hind legs, thus earning them the nickname gorildogs. As a species, their snouts elongated, their teeth increased in number, and their jaws developed the clamping power of a hydraulic vice. If they had once been pets, all compassion for their owners had been cleansed. They turned on their masters. Humans were a food source, and a gorildog's desire to eat was insatiable.

Felines had shed their fur. Though their bodies bloated to

twice their original size, their meat was toxic, even gorildogs shunned them. Spindly appendages resembling spider's legs with sharp barbs running along their length, sprang from their midsections. These mutated felines became known as spidlers.

Spidlers retained their feline quickness and curiosity, and their instinct to hunt became all-consuming. Spidlers were craftier after their exposure to the gray rain, but they retained their patience. Steel had heard of many a person who had been unaware that a spidler was tracking them until it was too late.

She had not thought much about how the bashers originated. The consensus in the shelter was that they were once cows, though none of them recalled ever having seen a cow in the city. Bashers were built like bulls on steroids, with a similar temperament. They were unbelievably strong, vicious, and single-minded. Nobody who had stumbled upon a basher in the open would live to tell the story. As far as she knew, they were the only animals impervious to the burning rain.

There may have been other animals that mutated when touched by the gray rain, but no one she knew had ever seen one. She often wondered how any of those monstrosities that survived the rains had managed to feed themselves. She'd come to the conclusion that, aside from the adults and any young people they came upon, they fed on each other.

Steel lamented that all of the birds had vanished. Mornings without their songs only served to reinforce the dread of her existence. The bite of a mosquito, the shooing of flies, and the sight of ants crawling along the ground were things of the past. If there were any insects remaining, they were hidden well underground.

The thought of ants awakened a memory in Steel from when she was a toddler. Her father had been pushing her on a swing when she had felt something crawling up her arm. Thinking it was a wasp, she panicked and let go of the ropes. She tumbled off the seat, falling harmlessly to the ground. Cringing, she turned her head away from her father and lifted her arm up for him to see. After a thorough inspection, he had laughed and pointed out that it was only an ant. She sat at the base of the old maple and had laughed along with him.

Now, all of the maples were gone.

There wasn't any plant life to speak of. Dead, scorched trees dotted the city and suburbs, their limbs missing or broken, their trunks decayed. Lawns, brush, and scrub had disappeared, burned to ash and blown away. The gray rain and the burning rain that followed affected only living matter, so shelter for those who survived was readily available. The young people who hadn't been killed managed to stay alive on canned food and bottled liquids.

It was during one of her scavenging missions for food that Wise had found her. By then, Steel had been on her own for three weeks.

When the gray rain first came, she had been home alone, as neither of her parents had returned from work. It was around suppertime when a breaking news report interrupted the show she had been watching. The newswoman was outdoors, standing under a concrete overhang as she read from a sheet of paper. She had been nervous, looking from side to side instead of at the camera, as if worried someone would approach her. The screen flickered and Steel had thought there must have been a problem with the power. She had been able to discern that the reporter was talking about some sort of odd precipitation that had begun to fall over the city. Through the static, Steel had also heard the woman say it was affecting people in strange and troubling ways. The newswoman's last words before the live feed turned to snow were to warn everyone to stay home, or if that were impossible, to take shelter from the rain.

Steel had run to her living room window, pulled the curtains aside and looked out over the street. The rain poured down.

The scene had been chaotic.

People were attacking each other, many of them bleeding so badly the heavy rain couldn't wash it away. She had watched helplessly as a neighbor—her friend Julie—had been pursued by a woman on all fours. Steel had gasped when she recognized the predator. It was Julie's mother.

The woman's agility and quickness had stunned Steel. It had taken only moments for the woman to catch up with her daughter, clamp her mouth around the young girl's neck, and tear through her skin. Julie's mother feasted.

Steel had run from the sight. She locked every door and window in the house, and when she had finished, she waited in the kitchen for whatever came next. She had been thinking of her parents, wondering when they were going to come and save her, when the assault came.

Loud thuds had boomed against the front and back doors. The sounds echoed throughout the house, bouncing off walls and ceilings as they made a determined path to her ears. Steel had slumped against the kitchen wall and closed her eyes. A refrain played over and over in her head: *Don't make any noise—don't make any noise.*

She tried to make a deal with God. *Make them go away,* she silently beseeched, *and I'll be good from now on. Really, I promise to be really, really good!* But the volume of the pounding had only increased.

Steel had raised her hands and placed the palms against her ears to block out the cacophony of hell at the doors. Whoever was out there, their blows had been too powerful, too insistent, and there was no sealing it out. She had slid down the wall, chest heaving from the sobbing she couldn't control. After she had reached the floor, a puddle had formed between her legs.

The window in her parents' bedroom imploded. The sound of the breaking glass had brought her close to a full panic. She had thought that this was it, the end for her. The crazy people would have her in moments. But she wasn't ready to die. She forced herself to calm down, and think.

Hiding in the cellar wasn't a good option. That door was flimsier than the front and back doors, and her attackers would break it down easily. Her only other choice had been the attic. She bolted to the second floor and paused in the hallway to look up at the ceiling. She had found what she was looking for: a skinny rope inching out from the ceiling and following the wall down to a peg. She unwound the rope from the peg and let the tension out. A ladder descended from the ceiling, and she scurried up, then pulled on the rope. Exhausted, she had lain next to the retracted ladder, scared and breathing heavily, still holding the end of the rope tight.

Steel had spent several days in the attic listening in fear as intruders, grunting like wild animals, had rummaged through her home. Hunger had eventually driven her from the confines of her hiding place, but only after listening, ear to the floor, for long periods to ensure she was alone in the house. She managed to live in that attic for weeks. When she thought it safe, she had snuck downstairs for food, raiding the refrigerator until there was nothing left. She had stayed away from the freezer as she dared not cook any meat, but hunger eventually led her back to it. She had taken only what she could thaw and eat raw in one sitting. After the electricity had failed, she refused to open the freezer, worried that the odor would attract them. Eventually, her stores had run out. The gray rains had stopped by then, and the burning rains had yet to arrive. Having no choice, she had ventured outdoors to scavenge.

She left the house only in the evenings, her hunger much stronger than her fear. With the power out, the absence of streetlights aided her in her bid to remain invisible. She dressed in dark clothes, stayed away from open areas, and darted from one car to another to keep out of sight. It was during one of those late-evening foraging missions when she had first crossed paths with Wise.

Steel's evening travels had taken her farther and farther away from home. Reluctant to go into the city, she had traveled south, to the more rural areas. Though there were fewer houses to scavenge, she had felt safer. One evening, her search for food had taken her close to the records storage facility.

The building was constructed of gray cinder block, three stories high, and ran the length and width of half a city block. It had reminded her of a post office. While a few of the first and second story windows had been broken, all of the third floor windows were shattered. She had expected to see security measures since it *was* a federal government facility, such as a barbed-wire fence, surveillance cameras, or a large steel door at the entrance, but none of these were in her view. She cautiously approached the building, moving through shadows when she could. When she got close enough, she took note of the broken panes of glass in the top portion of the wooden doors. On closer inspection, she discovered that the doors were ajar. The gap between them had looked as dark as the night sky above her. She had debated whether to enter the building. She doubted that there was any food remaining inside, but there might be weapons. Steel fought the urge to turn and leave. She understood it was foolish to take chances; there was no guarantee she would find anything worth keeping inside the building. Against reason, she stepped forward, but before her foot had made contact with the ground, a hand grasped her shoulder.

Her first instinct should have been to run like hell, but the lightness of the grip stayed the impulse. She froze, waiting for what was to come next—and when it came, a charge like electricity traveled through her body.

"Hello there, miss."

At the sound of another human's voice—a man's—Steel's knees went weak. She collapsed. Those were the first intelligent words she'd heard in weeks, and the relief that spread through her body was overwhelming. She had offered no resistance when his arms encircled her and held her upright. Steel had attempted to turn, to see who was behind her, but his hold made it impossible. When she felt her body being lowered gently to the ground, she knew she would have her chance soon. When her bottom made contact with the pavement, the grip on her loosened, and then withdrew completely. Out of the corner of her eye, she tracked him as he slowly walked around her to show himself. When she was face to face with him, Steel had been oblivious to everything else but his eyes. They were jade, and even in evening shadow, they shone as if they had been polished.

"Are you okay, miss?"

Steel knew he had expected an answer, but she hesitated. She recalled forcing herself to look away from his eyes to study the rest of his face. It had been too dark for her to take an adequate measure, but from what she saw there seemed to be a genuine look of concern. She knew right then that he had not changed. Satisfied for the moment that he wasn't a threat, she finally replied.

"I am. Thank you."

The young man had extended his hand. Steel reached for it and he pulled her up from the ground. Next came a short period of awkwardness, each waiting for the other to speak.

Steel broke the silence. "Why is all of this happening?"

His face went pale. He closed his eyes as he lifted his head. After a few moments of thought, his hand went to her shoulder. "Sometimes, we search for advantages in areas we should be forbidden to. There were answers to our problems all around us, there was no need to look elsewhere. What matters now is that we deal with—"

Their bodies stiffened and their eyes locked when they heard a rustling nearby.

"Come on," he'd said calmly, "we have to get out of here." He'd grabbed her hand and rushed them north, away from the facility.

"Why aren't we going inside?"

"It's too dangerous. There's nothing in there that can help us. We can go to my shelter where it's safe." The stranger then took her on a lengthy route, miles from the records facility to arrive at the shelter. That evening, she was introduced to Melancholy, Rock, Cookie, Ant, and Tool.

Ant had been an excellent climber and, like his namesake, he could scale almost any wall without fear. Tool had been the shelter's mechanic, able to repair almost anything that was worth repairing. Both had died shortly after Steel's arrival. Ant was killed by a spidler that had been lying in wait for him on a rooftop. His body was never recovered. Tool was crushed beneath the weight of a large generator he was attempting to fix in a nearby garage. No one knew why the winch that supported the generator had failed. There had been no sign of animals nearby, and Tool hadn't been picked over. Wise had discovered the body and had broken the news to the rest of them. While they were all saddened by the young boy's death, the group had eaten well that night.

Steel remembered one other thing about that evening. While they were eating, whenever she stole a glance at Wise, his eyes had been trained on her. Once, after she had held his gaze for longer than a moment, the thought came to her that those jade eyes held secrets. She recalled turning from him, looking down at her plate, and realizing that their bellies were full because of an unexplained accident in the garage.

*Secrets.*

"Huh? Steel, did you say something?"

Steel sat up quickly. Confused, she looked around, trying to get her bearings. When her head cleared a bit and her vision focused, she settled her eyes on Fleet. He stood by the side of her mattress, looking down with concern.

"Are you all right?"

Steel lifted her palms to her face. She rubbed her cheeks with force, and then used her fingers to sweep the sleep from her eyes. She tilted her head back, swiveling it in a circular motion, stretching her neck.

"Yeah, I must have dozed off."

"You've been out for over two hours. I thought I heard you say something so I came over to see if you were okay."

Annoyed, Steel dismissed him. "I'm okay. Get everyone together. You, me, and Rock are going to go out on a scavenging mission. We need food."

Though her words were garbled from yawning, Fleet had no trouble understanding her. "I figured that, but we'll have to go without Rock."

"What? Why?" Steel was wide awake now.

"He went out on his own. While you were out of it, the two of us went back to look for another automobile to place against the crack. We found a small one and pushed it back to the shelter. Afterward, he told me that he was going to go out on his own to look for some food. I tried to talk him out of it, to wait until you got up, but he insisted that you weren't up to the task. He wanted me to go with him but I refused—told him I wasn't going without you. He got pissed, said he was the only one with any balls around here, and that he was going to find us something to eat."

Steel felt the heat in her face rise, and wrinkled her brow. She stared hard at Fleet. "If we all get back tonight in one piece and still don't have any food, we're going to find out exactly what kind of balls Rock really has."

It took a moment for Fleet to digest what Steel had just said; when her implication finally sank in, he shuddered.

"Which direction did he go?"

"South."

Steel stiffened. She saw Fleet raise his eyebrows at her discomfort. After an awkward silence, she asked, "Where are Cookie and Daisy?"

Fleet jerked his thumb over his shoulder. Steel peered around him. The girls were standing by the dinner table. Both of them had wide eyes and pursed lips.

"Come here, you two."

They obeyed, trotting over to her as if their lives depended on it.

"I hate to do this, but we're going to have to leave you both here. Cookie, you're in charge while we're gone. Watch Daisy and don't let anyone into the shelter who isn't part of our group. And, I mean nobody! And, *don't* leave the shelter. Stay indoors. Make sure the door is latched and that you stay away from the windows. If Rock comes back, tell him to stay put. We'll be back before the burning rain."

Cookie trembled, but her reply was even and strong. "We'll be fine, Steel. Just make sure you come back." Daisy said nothing, but reached out a hand to Cookie, who grasped it tightly.

Steel stood and reached for her katana. After affixing its scabbard over her shoulder, she slipped another sheath containing an eight-inch knife into her belt loop. She adjusted it so it rested against her right hip, then stooped and slipped a paring knife into her left boot. Steel straightened and turned to Fleet. He had also armed himself: two short knives hung from holsters on his hips, and in his hand he carried a short-handled hatchet.

Stone-faced, Steel walked to the door, followed by the other three. As she opened it, she paused, turned, and addressed the girls. "Remember what I told you," she admonished Cookie, and then, looking at Daisy, she added with a smile, "we'll be back soon." She stepped outside with Fleet at her heels, stopping a couple of feet away until she heard the door latch. When the bolts had been thrown, she nodded to Fleet, and they began their journey south.

# CHAPTER FOUR

Steel and Fleet remained silent except for an occasional *hey* to alert the other to a path to take or an obstacle to avoid. A hand motion or a quick nod was sufficient for communication. Their silence was not only to safeguard against predators; it gave each of them time to climb into their own heads. Steel led the way. With the assurance of her stride and sense of direction, Fleet thought she had known their destination from the start. They had traveled this way in the past but the pickings had been slim. Why was Rock—and now Steel—headed south?

Fleet followed her through the empty streets feeling much like a younger sibling tagging along behind an older sister. For the most part, she ignored him. Fleet had no problem with that. Fascinated by the woman, he was content to simply be in her presence. A picture of Steel reaching her twenties intruded, and after hideous images of her turning insane flashed through his mind, he successfully shook the thought. They were all facing a death sentence, and it didn't pay to dwell on it.

Routinely, they scanned left and right as they scouted the various neighborhoods. Each had a role: Fleet looked for opportunities to find food; Steel watched for predators. While they hadn't found much in terms of sustenance or weapons on their earlier trips through this section of town, things appeared even worse now. The houses had all been ransacked, the doors torn from their jambs. Glass from broken windows littered the lawns. Some of the homes were close to completely destroyed with large holes in their walls and collapsed roofs. *Had to be the work of bashers,* thought Fleet. There were no bodies on the ground, but any adults and animals would have made quick work of those. The areas they passed through were once rural, residential neighborhoods, teeming with life. Now it resembled a war zone. There were no stores in sight, and Fleet recalled only one non-residential building on this side of town, a government building.

Fleet was tempted to break the silence. He wanted to ask Steel why they were headed in this direction, but suddenly things started to add up for him. He realized that they were on a very specific kind of hunt—that Steel had known all along where the food was. She was leading him to the Army's record storage facility, and that the only reason she would do so was because Steel believed Rock was there. The more he thought about where they were going—and why—the more his skin crawled.

Fleet decided to confront Steel. He quickened his pace until he was directly behind her. Before he could utter a word, she came to an abrupt halt, and he ran into her.

She turned and shot him a scowl. "What in the hell are you doing?" she whispered, sounding peeved.

In a low voice he replied, "I was going to ask you a question and you stopped suddenly. What's with that?"

Steel lowered her head, acting as if there were something interesting on the ground.

"I've got to go to the bathroom, and I can't wait any longer."

At one time, a girl telling him that she had to go to the bathroom would have turned his face red, but after living with a group of people in such close quarters for many months, Fleet was immune to embarrassment over bodily functions. After all the things he had seen, heard, and smelled in the shelter, he was surprised that she even bothered to tell him. "Yeah? Well, why are you standing there? Go behind a car or something."

She turned her head to him, but avoided looking into his eyes. "I want to use a real toilet. I'm tired of squatting over the ground or a bucket. And I want to feel toilet paper on my ass, not old newspapers or pages from some magazine."

Fleet was at a loss for words, but only for a moment. He could relate. Toilet paper was a scarce commodity; food was the priority on their salvaging missions, and everyone was expected to return with as much of it as possible. Toilet paper was a luxury. With a smile, he pointed to one of the empty houses and said, "You go on. I'll wait for you inside, by the front door, and keep an eye out until you're done."

Still avoiding eye contact, Steel nodded and they both walked over to what looked like a newly built ranch house. The doors were gone and the windows were smashed, but the walls and the roof were intact. They entered cautiously and did a sweep of the living room, bedrooms, and the kitchen area to be sure there was no adults or animals using the home for shelter. Satisfied that they were alone and secure, Fleet watched as Steel opened a door in one of the hallways and stepped into a bathroom. The first thing she did was check if there was toilet paper on the roll. He heard a chuckle, and the door slammed. Stifling a laugh, he hollered to her through the door that he would be waiting, then, he left her to do her business.

Fleet's eyes roamed the perimeter of the neighborhood as he stood in the doorway at the front of the house. Since the world had gone to hell, a light haze had claimed the skies during the daylight hours. It wasn't as bright outside as it used to be. Fleet's vision had adjusted to the change, but when it came to seeing objects at a distance, some days were better than others. Today the haze was lighter than it had been over the last few weeks so he had a decent view of his surroundings. While the sun was barely visible when the haze was thick, it had no effect on the heat—it continued to beat down unabated, drying the soil and preparing it for the evenings eventual soaking.

He felt the heat penetrating his skin. His forehead was dotted with beads of sweat and his clothes were sticking to him.

Fleet thought it close to midday, which didn't leave much time to find food and then hightail it back to the shelter. None of them wore watches so he wasn't sure what time it was. A few had owned them when they arrived but between their crystals breaking during chores, and batteries running out, watches didn't stay on wrists very long. Where the sun sat in the sky was their best gauge of time, but if its position couldn't be determined, instinct prevailed when it came time to do chores, seek shelter, and eat.

The thought of food reminded Fleet of his foraging mission with Steel. His unease returned.

If Steel was hunting for Rock and they found him at the records building, Fleet was unsure of what he would do. He had no love for the guy, despite Rock having saved his life that very morning. Rock had been a pain in the ass ever since Steel arrived all those months ago. From the moment Rock laid eyes on Steel, he hadn't bothered to conceal his desire. In the beginning it had been kind of cute—his sticking close to her, offering to help out with her chores, and trying to act manly in her presence. When those tactics had failed to endear him to her, his advances became more direct, forceful, and awkward. They all could see that Steel had been uncomfortable around him, and she soon shunned him, finding any excuse to avoid his presence.

Rejected, Rock had turned desperate. He had changed tactics, ignoring her and depriving her of his company. She would miss him, he had confided to Fleet, and see the error of her ways. Rock had thought himself special since Steel had slept with him not long after she first arrived at the shelter. But he hadn't counted on her independent streak—her will was as strong as the metal Wise had named her after. No sooner than Rock pulled his "I'm too good for you" act, Steel slept with all the boys who were old enough, including Fleet.

Wise never interfered or commented on Steel's sexual exploits, giving the group the impression that he condoned it. Fleet wasn't sure what the relationship had been between Steel and Wise—they were often as volatile with each other as they had been intimate. As complicated as it was, there was no denying that Steel benefited more than Wise from the relationship. Despite her bed-hopping, Wise had been the only male she had showed a genuine love for. From the way her gaze had rested on Wise when he wasn't looking, to the respect she proffered him in front of others, it wasn't difficult to notice the depth of her feeling for the man.

After Wise had passed on, Rock assumed he'd be in charge; Steel would have no choice but to show the same respect for him as she did Wise. It hadn't worked out that way. To different degrees, all of them had been affected by Wise's death, but Rock was the only one who not only accepted it, but seemed glad for it.

When Wise died, something inside of Steel did, too. She'd stopped sleeping with any of them, and her emotions had turned as hard as her will.

Nightmares kept the memories of the night Wise died sharp in Fleet's mind. Earlier that evening, Wise had been discussing something with Steel in one corner of the shelter. Fleet remembered the two of them sitting stiffly in their chairs, their conversation hushed but filled with tension. Fleet had never seen Steel as afraid, confused, or depressed as she'd been that evening. Though never the type to walk around with a smile on her face or chat any of them up, she was usually pleasant enough to put them all at ease when she was near. But that night, as she and Wise conferred in the corner, Fleet had seen a different side of Steel. Her face was drawn and pale, and her upper body sagging as if a weight had been placed on her shoulders. The two of them had talked for a good half hour, with Steel often shaking her head, and occasionally glancing in Rock's direction. Fleet recalled feeling lethargic that night. He had been tired from foraging for food, and hungry as a result of not finding any, so he'd sat in a chair by the lantern and tried to follow their conversation from a distance. Wise and Steel had been so engrossed in their conversation they hadn't realized they were being observed.

The discussion ended abruptly. Wise had stood and walked toward a small table at the north wall of the shelter. Steel remained where she sat, slightly slumped over and unmoving, though her eyes followed Wise's progress. When he had reached the wall, he turned and leaned back against it. By this time, all of the others in the shelter had realized something was up, and they turned to face him.

The room went silent.

Without a word, Wise had removed his clothes, stripping down until he was completely naked. He picked up the discards and tossed them a few feet away. They all watched Wise undress with interest, but without the energy to question him—they were as listless and weak as Fleet. Wise glanced at each of them, one at a time, as if committing their faces to memory, then, he motioned for them to come closer. All of them, including Steel, obeyed, and they formed a semicircle around Wise, their faces lean and curious, but not alarmed.

Wise then reached over to the table and picked something up. He made a tight fist around it, and brought it up to his chest. When he opened his fist, they all saw it was a knife, about eight inches long, its blade smooth and glinting in the light of the lantern. He swung his other hand up, grabbing the hilt and holding it tightly. He lifted the knife higher, to just above his head. Wise turned, right to left, gazing at each of them briefly, though he lingered on Steel for a few extra moments. Finally, he lifted his chin slowly until his eyes rested on the knife. Then, with a motion that was as deliberate as it was quick, Wise brought the knife down and plunged it into his lower belly.

Not one of them said a word.

Not one of them made a move toward him.

Intuitively, they had all understood what was happening. Their facial expressions hadn't changed the slightest during or after the stabbing—they hadn't so much as cringed. Their mouths remained closed. Not a gasp was exhaled nor a groan uttered. They had watched impassively, not in horror or anticipation. No, Fleet recalled, *we all simply stood there like patient dogs waiting for a meal.*

The blade had sunk into Wise's stomach to the hilt. He held it securely in his blood- drenched hands, as if he were afraid to let it go. A gasp escaped his lips, but he remained standing. He collected himself, gathering the strength needed to finish what he'd started. But, when he had tried to pull up on the knife to finish the job, the pain must have been too much for him. Finally, he let it go, dropping both his hands to his sides. His breathing became heavy, gulping air in an attempt to keep it in his lungs. Blood flowed from the wound in rivulets, catching on his pubic hair and soaking it crimson before dripping down onto his penis and then the floor. In agony, Wise turned his head toward Steel, and their eyes locked. He stared at her, letting Steel register his pain, and then he nodded. She returned the stare and, after a moment of hesitation, she nodded back.

Steel rose, walked over to Wise, and stood before him, gazing deeply into his eyes without emotion. Without breaking eye contact, she placed both of her hands on the hilt of the knife, finishing what Wise had started. The knife slipped through skin and muscle easily—she pulled it all the way up to his breastbone.

Wise's head jolted backward: they all heard the crack as it hit the wall. He released a small sigh before his legs gave out, slipping toward the floor. Steel released her hold on the knife and gripped his shoulders, easing him gently down the wall. He came to rest on his rear end, legs splayed out in front of him. Steel withdrew the knife and made more cuts without bothering to ensure that Wise was dead. When finished, she pulled at both sides of the wound, exposing his chest cavity. His intestines spilled onto the floor.

Fleet couldn't—or chose not to—remember the specifics of what had occurred after that. But, he did recall that everyone in the shelter went to bed with full bellies that night.

With only one exception, no one objected when, five days after Wise died, Steel announced that she was taking over the leadership of the shelter.

As Fleet stood in the doorway now, sweating and waiting for Steel to finish up, his stomach rumbled. It was the thought of food. It served to distract him from his thoughts of Wise's death. He turned to look back into the house, wondering if Steel was out of the bathroom yet. She had been in there for a long time, more than enough for her to finish her business. Panic wormed its way into his thoughts. What if Steel had left the house? That whole "having to go to the bathroom" thing was a ruse? What if she had been trying to lose him?

Could she have been so determined to kill Rock that she would abandon him, thinking maybe that he would have tried to stop her?

Fleet left his position at the entrance and made his way to the bathroom. The door was closed. "Steel? You done yet?" No answer. "Steel, you in there?" Still nothing.

Fleet's panic turned to anger. He couldn't believe she would just leave him! He lunged for the doorknob, twisted it and pulled the door open. He was all set to turn away, pissed off and frustrated if the bathroom was empty. Instead, he froze.

Steel was still in the bathroom. She was sitting on the toilet, pants down by her ankles, elbows resting on her knees propping her head up as if she were bored. Her katana leaned against the wall to her right. Fleet's face turned red at his foolishness. He began stammering out an apology but stopped short. The look in her eyes told him something was wrong. They were wide, and she was staring at something hard enough to bore a hole through it.

Her eyes were aimed off to her left, not on him. Confused, he followed their direction.

A few feet away from Steel was the biggest spidler he had ever seen.

It was perched on the rim of the bathtub, the upper part of its body leaning over the top with two of its front legs in the air, quivering, ready to strike. Two of its other legs were holding onto the curved rim for purchase. The remainder of the spidler was out of sight, but Fleet could hear the sounds of its lower legs slipping against the tub's sleek walls as it attempted to climb out.

Fleet could only gawk at the beast for a few seconds, unsure of what to do. In desperation, he whispered to Steel, "Don't move."

He felt like an idiot. Of course, she wasn't going to move—she probably hadn't moved a muscle since she sat down and saw the damn thing. Spidlers, like cats, were mainly interested in moving objects. They liked to play with their food before eating it. First, they would stab one of their leg barbs into their prey, injecting a fast-acting paralytic. Then they would retreat and wait a few moments to have their fun. Had that happened already? What if Steel had been stung and was too paralyzed to move? Another look into her eyes told him that was not the case. She was alert, just scared to death. Something else occurred to him. By opening the door, he just put himself in play. Any quick movement on his part would send the spidler after Steel. Or him.

Fleet remained still. There was only one way to get Steel out of this jam. He would have to make the spidler come after him, but the idea of this creature coming anywhere closer to him made him want to throw up. He knew he was fast. That's why Wise had named him Fleet in the first place; but he also knew that spidlers were faster. He had a lot to lose if things didn't go his way.

"Pssst—pssst." Fleet tried to get her attention.

Steel's eyes turned toward him. So did the spidler's.

Turning his head slightly toward the katana, Fleet moved his eyes back and forth between Steel and her sword. She squinted—a signal that she had no idea what he was trying to tell her. He let his eyes rest on hers and then he mouthed the words, "Get ready." Though she must've had no idea what he was up to, her eyes softened with trust. Then almost imperceptibly, she nodded.

Sighing inwardly, Fleet slowly turned to the spidler. The creature noticed the motion. In less time than it took Fleet to blink his eyes, it moved, facing him. Fleet stifled a gasp. Shaking, he doubted he had the nerve to do what he needed to. Both stood their ground in the bathroom, one of them shaking in fright, the other waiting to strike. They stared at each other for an eternity. One of them decided to end the standoff.

Fleet ran like hell to the entrance of the house.

He made it three feet away from the bathroom when something brushed against his legs. Looking down, he saw the spidler clamping itself around his right calf. Fleet screamed at the top of his lungs as he fell facedown onto the floor. Turning over as fast as he could, he lifted his head and saw that the spidler was crawling up his leg.

Never having seen one up close, Fleet was struck by how feline the creature's face was. It had short whiskers, pointed ears, and a button nose. The mouth was all wrong, though: it was way too large for a cat. And—there were all those teeth.

Fleet never would have thought it possible for a cat to smile, even if it *did* have insect-like legs, but he would swear that's what the damned thing was doing.

The creature scurried past Fleet's groin and over his stomach. It came to rest on his chest.

The spidler raised its front two legs. They quivered. Fleet closed his eyes and waited for it to strike. When it came, the spidler struck like lightning. The barbs cut deeply, precisely, and sliced both sides of his neck.

Fleet's eyes bulged when he felt the sting. The pain was intense at first, but soon ebbed. The paralytic worked instantly— the blood he could feel running down his neck went from a tickle to his not feeling it at all. He stared at the creature. The spidler's smile appeared wider.

Fleet tried to look away, but he couldn't move. He struggled against the paralytic, but his muscles would not respond. Frozen, he stared into the face of the creature that was going to kill him.

A motion, too quick to identify, flashed before him. Liquid splashed in his eyes, blinding him. Fleet was grateful he couldn't feel any pain. His thoughts were on Steel as he waited for death.

Moments later, he saw a white cloth going in and out of his vision.

The cloth vanished and a face came into view. It was Steel. She was so close he could have counted the pores on her nose.

"Fleet, you okay?"

To his surprise, his lips parted slightly. Somehow he got out the words, "Yeth; can't moove dough."

It took Steel a few seconds to figure out what Fleet was trying to say. She pulled away from him and straightened up, stepping back a few paces.

Fleet's eyes were also regaining some mobility and they followed her. Steel was grinning. Lowering his eyes, he saw the katana, held tightly in her right hand, dripping blood. Her other hand held a white cloth stained red.

Steel shrugged. "I cut its head off."

Dropping his eyes, Fleet saw that her pants were still around her ankles. It took some effort, but Fleet managed to smile.

Acknowledging the smile in kind, Steel used her katana to push what remained of the spidler off Fleet's chest. Turning, she balanced the sword up against the wall. She inspected the bloody cloth in her hand and then tossed it aside. She took off her sneakers and removed her pants. "Be right back," she muttered, then quickly proceeded to the bathroom, went inside, and closed the door.

*Well, that answers one question,* thought Fleet.

While Steel did her business, Fleet tried to move various body parts. Initially nothing responded, but after some effort, he felt his muscles coming to life again. He had progressed to wiggling his fingers and toes when he heard the sound of the toilet lid hitting the seat. Steel emerged from the bathroom. Without so much as a glance at him, she grabbed her pants. She left his field of vision to put them on and then sauntered back into his view. She casually picked up her sneakers and, balancing herself on one foot at a time, slipped them on without bothering to untie them first.

Steel made eye contact with Fleet, then walked over to him. She stepped one leg over him, straddling his chest. Looking up, it occurred to Fleet that the view might be more pleasurable if she were wearing a skirt. Before he could take that fantasy any further, she sat on his chest. Though he could barely feel her, Fleet knew that she wasn't putting all her weight on him—he had no trouble breathing.

Steel leaned over until their noses were an inch apart. To Fleet's amazement, she turned her head up slightly and planted a kiss on his lips. "You saved my life, Fleet."

Fleet thanked God that he was able to feel the kiss. He thought he could also feel another of his extremities coming back to life.

Steel straightened up and peered down at him, her face solemn. "Now, I've got some bad news for you."

Fleet thought he knew what was coming.

"I've got to keep moving and you're in no condition to come along. I'm going to leave you here while I go and hunt up some food."

Fleet noticed that she'd used the word, *hunt.*

"I'm going to put you in one of the bedrooms and lock the door. I've no idea how long it's going to take you to get back to normal, but I'm hoping you'll at least be able to walk by the time I get back—and believe me, I have every intention of coming back for you. But if something happens to me or I'm delayed, use your own judgment on leaving. I figure it'll take you at least a couple of hours to get back to the shelter before the rain starts, maybe more if you're still weak. It would be nice if at least one of us was there, but they should be okay for the night if we don't get back in time."

Fleet couldn't argue with Steel's logic. She didn't bother waiting for a response anyway. Steel stood up quickly and did a shuffle to get behind his head. She lifted him up under his arms and dragged him to an empty bedroom, leaving him on the floor next to the bed, placing a pillow under his head. At the bedroom door she paused and glanced back at him. Fleet thought she was going to say something else. Instead, she approached him. Steel bent down on one knee and kissed him, this time on his forehead. Smiling, she thanked him again and left the room without looking back.

When the door closed, Fleet went to work on trying to get his body to move.

# CHAPTER FIVE

Steel's gaze swept the front of the US Army's record storage facility. She thought it even less impressive than the first time she'd seen it. In daylight, gray paint peeled from the cinder blocks, as did the white paint on the window trim that dotted the three floors of the building. The jagged edges of glass on the third floor windows looked untouched from the last time she was here. She took a moment to peer through all the windows for any signs of life, maybe a face peering back at her or an unusual shadow. She didn't spot anything. She raised her shoulders and shook off the tension.

*Rock has to be here.*

She slipped the katana out of its sleeve, grasped it tightly in her right hand, and walked toward the entrance at the south corner of the building.

The doors were open wider than the last time. Not wide enough for a basher, but a spidler could easily fit through its two-foot gap. So could a person. *It's an invitation*, she thought. *Rock knew I would come for him*. With the tip of her katana leading the way, she stepped through the gap.

There was enough sunlight streaming in through the windows that Steel had a good view of the interior. Her earlier impression, that the building resembled a post office, changed now that she was inside: a warehouse might have been a more apt description.

Beyond the entrance doors, Steel had to pass beneath an arch. It was high and wide enough for two people to walk through. It was metallic, and rust had taken root along its surface. A metal detector—the only sign of security she had seen so far. Past the arch, she entered a large area that ran about thirty feet wide and ninety feet to the back of the building. Support beams, spaced wide and uniformly, snaked up from the floor and passed through the ceiling. Ten feet beyond the metal detector, a service counter ran the width of the foyer. The countertop was bare, except for a few posters taped to its front, explaining various government safety rules, regulations, and warnings. Behind the counter, dozens of wooden desks took up the space. They were plain, made from a dark-hued wood, and they looked solidly built. All of them were aligned in perfect rows—so fastidiously arranged, she couldn't help but wonder if their legs had been bolted to the floor. There were no computers or phones cluttering their surfaces—not a tape dispenser, stapler, pens, paper or inbox basket in sight.

Steel stood before the counter, looked left and gazed past the desks toward the north end of the building. Rows of metal shelving units ran the length and width of the floor space. They were set up library style—ten aisles with five feet of space between them. The aisles began at the edge of the foyer and extended to the far wall. All of the shelves, at least as far as she could see, held white rectangular boxes, all identical in size and all capped with black covers.

To her right, she saw a stairway, painted a shade of beige. It also showed signs of age. The stairs were uneven—both ends of the steps were worn down so much they looked as if every tread frowned at her. The handrail sagged between supports, and she made a mental note not to test its ability to support her weight. The stairway began on the first floor.

*Does this building have a basement?*

Time wasn't on Steel's side. She had to decide which way to go: should she venture into the bowels of the shelving and peer into the boxes—or should she head upstairs? Nighttime would arrive in a couple of hours and she had not brought a lantern. She decided to forgo investigating the first floor and walked to the stairway.

At the stairs, Steel saw two faint sets of footprints in the thin layer of dust coating the treads. Though she couldn't tell which way they were headed, her heart skipped a beat. *Had Rock already been here and gone?* A renewed sense of urgency spurred her on and she climbed the stairway with spidler-like stealth. At the second floor landing, she paused and looked around.

Aisles, made up of shelving and boxes identical to the ones on the first floor, stretched from the stairway to the other end of the building. Despite the pristine look of the shelves, Steel's hand went to her katana. *Had anyone actually worked in this building?* She took a few steps closer and gazed down the aisle. Her eyes rested on the boxes closest to her. Though the boxes had yellowed slightly, they appeared to be in like-new condition. Each had a small label on the front, bright white in color and computer generated with a ten-digit number printed on them.

Steel squatted, the tip of her katana drawing a line through the dust on the floor. She reached over and struggled with the weight of a box off the lower shelf. It was too heavy so she slid it out, dropping it to the floor with a thud. Her nose twitched when dust flew into the air. After waving a hand to disperse it, she removed the cover and set it aside. Her eyes narrowed when she saw the contents—blank, unopened reams of 8 1/2 x 11" copy machine paper. She removed the top bundles and discovered that the box was crammed with more of the same. Confused, she checked the next carton. The identification number was one digit higher than the one she had opened. She slid that one out, and it, too, dropped onto the floor in a cloud of dust. Opening it, she found that it also contained only unopened reams of copy paper. She faced the opposite aisle and repeated the process. Working her way down and then over to the other aisles, box after box yielded the same results.

She stared at the mess littering the floor and tried to collect her thoughts. Everything she had seen since entering the building was too perfect. It was all window dressing.

*Wise had worked in this building. What in the hell did he do here?*
Steel walked back to the stairs and climbed to the third floor.

# CHAPTER SIX

The two young girls cowered in the center of the shelter, their foreheads pressed together and their arms wrapped around each other. They clung so tightly, Cookie snapped one of Daisy's ribs. Ear-piercing screams punctuated their whimpers.

Tables and chairs tumbled over and skidded across the concrete floor as if riding invisible waves. Every hanging weapon, utensil and decoration jackhammered against the walls as chunks of concrete rained down from the ceiling. The sound from all this madness was deafening, and it would have easily drowned out the girl's pleas for help—if anyone were around to hear them.

As terrified as the two girls were, their minds refused to shut down. With each jarring thud, with every piece of ceiling that fell, their fear only intensified. Adrenalin raced like bullets through their bodies and any chance they had of surrendering to unconsciousness was buried deep beneath their screams. The girls' panic appeared to have no threshold where it could peak and short-circuit their brains. With their fear escalating, they dug their nails into the other's back, as if trying to create an opening large enough to crawl inside and hide.

With mind-numbing rapidity, a basher pummeled their shelter.

When the attack started, the beast went at the building from the east, smashing into it several times, but unable to gain access. Systematically, it began to circle the shelter, ramming its massive head into different sections along the walls as it made its way around the building. This, too, went without success—until it came upon the automobile.

Though it was well known that bashers were capable of simple reasoning, this one could not have understood that the machine was placed against the building for a purpose. It had targeted the vehicle out of frustration, pounding away at it until it was ripped to pieces. When the beast took a moment to reassess its plan of attack after having demolished the car, it discovered the crack in the wall. It had no problem understanding this was the shelter's weakness.

The basher stepped away from the building, lowered its head, and assaulted the crack with a fury. It rammed the wall so hard, after each strike the beast bounced back at least a foot. Over and over again it rushed, putting every pound of its muscle into smashing its skull against the concrete. Oblivious to the pain, indifferent to anything else but its objective, the beast was the perfect battering ram.

When the basher broke through, it was taken by surprise. The crack had not only continued to lengthen from the pounding, but spread vertically in uneven fissures. As the basher backed up to prepare for another charge, the wall partially crumbled, leaving a large dust-filled gap. Unaware of its success, the beast sped toward the wall, easily plowing through the opening and entering the shelter at full throttle. Unable to stop, it careened into the path of the two girls.

Daisy was hit hard. She rolled head over heels, tumbling along the floor until she came to a stop against Steel's bed. She cried out in pain, but she was startled into silence when she found she was unable to move her legs. Glancing down, she saw they were twisted into unnatural positions. In a daze, she turned back to Cookie.

The weight of the basher, combined with the kicking of its powerful legs, had crushed and then pulverized Cookie into a pulpy mass. Blood pooled beneath her body, and Daisy saw her friend's head tilted back at an impossible angle. Cookie's severed arms lay by her knees, her hands still clinched. To Daisy, it looked as if the young girl had been praying.

After slamming into the two girls, the basher's momentum

continued until it crashed into the shelter's back wall. Unfazed by the collision, it paused to get its bearings. The beast lifted its massive head, turning it from side to side, garnering a larger view of its surroundings. It discovered that the food closest to it was dead—it could remain there for the time being. The food farthest away was still alive, though wounded. It would be dealt with first.

The beast snorted, lumbering toward its next meal.

Daisy didn't hear the footfalls of the approaching basher. She looked away from Cookie and turned her attention to her legs, willing them somehow to mend so she could stand and run. She felt the tickle of the beast's hot breath on her face and lifted her head. All she could see was a wall—so close that she had trouble focusing on it. The wall was wrinkled and dark, with the texture of leather. Then it began to move slowly upward, creating the illusion that she was sinking, being sucked down into the concrete floor. Her confusion ended abruptly as a slit in the wall rose into view; the movement ceased when the slit was level with her eyes.

The slit opened wide.

The last things Daisy saw in her short life were rows and rows of teeth.

# CHAPTER SEVEN

As Steel climbed the stairwell, the charade by the building's occupants monopolized her thoughts. She wondered how many people were needed to keep up the masquerade. Her musing was cut short when the tip of her boot stubbed against one of the stair risers. She fell forward, and the tip of her katana embedded itself into one of the stair treads. After pulling it out and inspecting the tip for damage, she was aware of how dark the stairway had become. Satisfied that she hadn't blunted the katana, she placed it back into its sheath and advanced to the top, where she found a closed door blocking access to the third floor. There was no landing leading to the door—the stairs simply ended at its base.

The door was as wide as the stairway, and it stretched to the ceiling. It was painted dark, possibly gray; she had a hard time discerning the color in the poor light. At its center, there was a wheel, reminding her of a submarine door. Above the wheel, there was an outline of a small rectangle. She thought it might be an observation window, but that didn't make sense, as it was blacked out.

After studying the door for a few seconds, Steel concluded she would have to push it open. That was unusual: in all of the industrial buildings the group had scavenged, the doors leading to exits or stairways had always swung out from the work area. Wise had explained to her that it was for safety reasons. If there was a fire in a building and a mob of people rushed the door, it would be nearly impossible for those closest to the door to pull it open with the crowd pushing from behind. It was one more oddity of the building to add to her list.

Steel expected the door to resist her efforts, but when she placed her hands on the wheel, she exhaled with relief—it spun freely. Her sense of ease did not last long. She heard no latch sliding or gears turning. She pressed against the door, and it floated easily away from her. When there was an opening large enough for her to sidle through, she grabbed the wheel to stop the door's momentum. She placed one arm against the doorjamb for support, and poked her head through the opening.

The third floor was different from the others.

A huge hole in the ceiling, perfectly round, about fifteen feet in diameter, extended through the roof. The fading daylight through the hole was enough for her to get an adequate view of the layout.

Steel slipped through the door and scanned the area. While the third floor also contained racks, there were far fewer of them, and all of them positioned against the walls. Most of the floor space was empty except for a few scattered desks, and there were a handful more in the center of the room. All of the desks had books and computers stacked atop them. The desks in the center were placed in a circle, positioned beneath the perimeter of the hole in the ceiling.

Steel gazed up at the hole, then back down at the circle of desks. There must have been something damned interesting going on for someone to arrange the desks in this pattern.

*Maybe they were circling the wagons.*

Steel skirted the center of the floor and headed toward the racks. Instead of boxes, these were filled with a collection of variously sized and bound books, reminding her of a library. Some of them appeared to be old, possibly antique, while others had smooth, glossy bindings. She stepped closer to read a few of the titles: *The Dai Vernon Book of Magic* by Luis Ganson; *Isn't It Wonderful?* by Charles Bertram; and *The Odin Rings* by Victor Farelli.

Steel took *The Odin Rings* off the shelf and opened it. It had a copyright date of 1931. It was in much better condition than some of the others, and it made her curious as to just how old some of these were. She placed it back on the shelf and walked farther down, reading the titles as she passed. The racks contained nothing but books devoted to magic, folklore, and conjuring. Many appeared to be valuable with covers made of exotic materials. She stopped to study one with a rich leather cover. The title on its spine simply read *The Old One*. It did not list an author. She reached for it, but before her fingertips could settle on the binding, she froze. She heard a footstep behind her.

Steel turned, both of her hands reaching for the katana as she spun. By the time her spin was complete, the sword was out of its sheath, fully extended and pointed toward the sound.

The source stood by the circle of desks. He held a rifle, its barrel pointed at her.

"Hello, Steel."

Steel looked hard at the gunman. "Hello, Rock."

"Put the katana down on the floor, and then we'll talk."

Steel hesitated, but only for a moment. She had no choice. She slowly lowered the katana to the floor.

Using the tip of his rifle, Rock pointed to one of the desks in the circle near him. "Sit down over here."

When Steel reached the desks, she peered over them, and let out an audible gasp.

Rock smiled. "Sure is something, ain't it?"

Where the floor should have been was a solid black circle. It was the same size as the hole in the ceiling. Its surface was dense, smooth, and glossy.

Looking back at Rock, Steel asked, "What is it?"

In response, Rock sat on top of a desk with his back to the stairway and picked up a book. He threw it at the circle. A corner of the book touched the surface of the circle and froze upright on contact, as if someone had hit a pause button.

With a furrowed brow, she looked back at Rock.

"That," began Rock, his eyes on the black circle, "is what killed the world."

He had spoken the words evenly, without emotion, so she couldn't discern if he was joking or entirely serious. His expression, however, was easier to read—he wore a frown. Were memories of a distant time playing in his head? If so, it was a side of Rock she hadn't seen. She found herself feeling a small measure of sympathy toward him.

Sighing, he lifted his head. "Before you came along, Wise and I spent a lot of time together. We usually paired up on foraging missions, so we got to know each other pretty well. Over time, we built a trust between us. He told me things about the work they did here. And, let me tell you, Steel, most of what he said was incredible! After I showed an interest in his stories—and that's what I thought they were, *stories*—he showed me things to prove he wasn't making them up. He brought me here, and told me how he had created that thing—that black circle in front of you—that black hole that killed the world."

Steel leaned forward and let her guard down a bit, trusting that Rock was not only telling the truth, but that he might have some real knowledge about why the world was so screwed up.

"Wise worked here as a researcher. He wasn't in charge or anything though—just an intern. The way he told it, there was a woman who ran the place, a Captain Holden. Wise said she was way too laid back and way too naïve to be running an operation like the one they had here."

Rock looked over to the racks and murmured something Steel couldn't hear.

Steel thought that Rock's mind was drifting, so she prodded him. "What kind of operation, Rock? And what did Wise mean when he said the woman was naïve?"

With the gun still trained on Steel, Rock swept his gaze around the third floor. "Look around you, Steel. What do you see? Books. Loads and loads of books. I saw you gazing at some of them, so I know you've already got an idea of what kind they are."

Pretending to scan the racks, Steel took note of how far away her katana was, trying to figure out how quickly she could reach it when the time came. Movement off to her right side, in the far corner of the floor, caught her attention. But, when she turned to look there was nothing there. Whatever it was, it was fast, and swallowed by the shadows. Steel didn't think that any person or any animal had come through the door since her arrival, so she reasoned that whatever it was must have been there before she had arrived. It was so fast that she thought it might be a spidler. She turned to Rock, wondering if he had caught the movement, but he didn't seem to have noticed anything unusual as he continued to wait for her response.

"The occult," she finally answered. "They are all books that deal with the supernatural."

"Yeah," he nodded. "Wise was with a group in the CIA that handled paranormal events. He wasn't someone who investigated odd occurrences like in that old TV show. He was strictly a researcher. They would send him and a few others in his team all over the world to pick up any books or literature they could find on the supernatural and bring them back here to analyze. You'd be amazed at what's sitting on those shelves. One day after searching for something in Salt Lake City, he was driving south and stopped for lunch in this small town called Spring Valley. He spotted an old bookstore and went inside to look around. That's where he found this."

Taking his eyes off Steel, Rock reached to the desk with one hand, grabbed something and held it up.

It was a small leather pamphlet tied together with rawhide strings. There was also a crude drawing on the cover but Steel was too far away to make it out.

"It's some kind of scrapbook, Steel, put together way back in the eighteen-hundreds by some Indian Chief named Long Elk. Wise wasn't sure of its value or even if it had any connection to his work, but he said something drew him to buy it. He couldn't understand the notations in it so he brought it back here, along with some of the other books he'd picked up in Salt Lake, and left it on his desk. Then he forgot about it. Weeks later, he came across it and decided to scan it into the agency's computer. He told me the computer was programmed with every known language from both ancient and modern times, and it could translate almost anything they fed into it. After inputting the information, the computer did its job and spit out a translation. When Wise read it, his curiosity was piqued, and he took it to Holden.

"Wise told me she was dismissive of the translation. She told him to file it along with all the other translations they had on early American Indian occult history and forget about it. When he took it back to his desk, something about it wouldn't stop picking at him. He went through and read one of the translated passages aloud. It made no sense to him, and he eventually put the book down on the corner of his desk with the thought of studying it later on. About an hour had passed when a hand grabbed his shoulder. It was Holden's, and she looked pale. She motioned for him to look at a spot on the floor about ten feet behind him. He did, and was confused by what he saw. A dark circle, about a yard across, had materialized in the middle of the floor."

Steel interrupted. "Three feet wide? That circle is a lot bigger than three feet wide!"

"Yeah," replied Rock, "It grew."

# CHAPTER EIGHT

Fleet leaned against a tree as he surveyed the front of the records building. The trip from the house had taken a toll on him, and though he was regaining his strength, he had just about worn himself out getting here. Thankfully, the spidler's venom was not as potent as he had expected, and he was able to raise himself to a standing position not long after Steel had left. His lack of strength and coordination, not to mention constantly being on guard for predators, slowed him down considerably, giving him way too much time to worry about her. The worst part, however, was his self-doubt. He wrestled with his decision to follow Steel instead of heading back to the shelter to stay with the girls. He didn't like the idea of leaving Cookie and Daisy alone, but he thought they would be secure in the shelter, and if anyone needed help it would be Steel. There was also the off chance Rock wasn't leading them on a wild-goose chase—maybe he was telling the truth about looking for food. If so, he would have returned to the shelter by now. Deep down, Fleet knew that wasn't the case. Steel was sure that Rock would head here, and she knew the guy better than anyone.

A prolonged study of the entrance convinced Fleet the area was clear of predators. He made his way to it and stepped through the front doors. Once inside, he passed through an arch, and then stood at a long counter. He looked around, listening, and heard nothing. The light was so dim he couldn't see the far reaches of the floor. Soon it would be too dark to see anything at all. Knowing his time was limited and seeing nothing that screamed for his attention, Fleet began to climb the stairs.

When he came to the second floor, he again checked for any

signs of Steel or Rock. Finding none, he kept moving.

As he approached the third floor, he saw a partially open door at the top of the stairs. He stopped at the top step, leaned toward the door, turned his head sideways, and listened.

His pulse quickened when he heard Rock's voice saying, "Yeah. It grew."

Fleet crouched low and peeked around the door.

# CHAPTER NINE

Steel kept a straight face when she saw Fleet poke his head around the stairway door.

Rock followed her glance and looked toward the stairs, but Fleet had already ducked out of sight. Seeing nothing unusual, Rock calmly turned back to Steel. "Nobody's coming to save you—it's just us."

Steel needed to keep Rock's attention on her, to give Fleet a chance to reach them before he was discovered. "Can I see that scrapbook?" she asked, motioning to the pamphlet still in his hand.

Rock appeared amused: his eyes lit up and the corners of his mouth stretched wide. "Maybe you think you can reverse what's happened, Steel? Or even stop the burning rain that comes every night? I've gone through the translation over and over. If there's a way to change things, I can't find it. But, hey, we got some time. See for yourself."

As Rock went to toss the scrapbook to her, Steel slid off the desk and approached him.

"Hey!" Rock warned, motioning with the rifle.

"I was just going to take it from you," she replied, continuing toward him.

When she was within a few feet of the rifle, Rock yelled, "Stop!"

Steel complied and he tossed her the scrapbook. Catching it, she opened the book and scanned the pages.

"Do you have the translation?" she asked.

Rock nodded and, while keeping an eye on her, he searched around the desktop.

While Rock was looking for the translation, Fleet poked his head around the door again. He inched his way through and took short, silent steps toward Rock.

Worried that Fleet might be heard, Steel engaged Rock in conversation to further distract him. "Did anyone go into the circle?" she asked.

Rock didn't respond right away, still searching for the translation while keeping Steel in his line of sight. Rock leaned sideways and extended his arm further, letting his fingers dance around the desk until they touched a small pile of papers. After sneaking a look, he made a quick nod and picked them up. "No, they never got the chance," he finally answered. "Wise told me about all their experiments. They threw pens, pencils, and books at it but they all landed on the top of the circle and stayed put. Captain Holden even walked on it, but her heel stuck to the surface and they had to slip her shoe off to release her. They couldn't figure out what the damned thing was. Then, Wise suggested that they might be looking at it all wrong. Maybe, it was designed opposite to what they thought—that it was made to let something out, not in. That's when—"

Rock never got to finish the sentence.

Fleet punched him in the back of the head as hard as he could. Rock's upper body flew forward from the blow, the translation flying out of his hand.

While Rock toppled toward the floor, Steel jumped back, scrambling to reach her katana. The move saved her life. She didn't know if it was a reaction to getting hit, but Rock's finger squeezed the trigger. The bullet would have passed right through her if she had remained where she was.

When Rock hit the floor, the rifle tumbled out of his hand. Fleet grabbed the gun and stood over Rock, pointing it at his head. Steel swept her katana off the floor and rushed toward them. As Rock struggled to rise, she placed the tip of the sword against his back.

"Easy," she warned.

Rock stood slowly, and reached for the desk. Head hung low, he massaged the back of his neck as he steadied himself. After a few moments, he sat down wincing. He remained quiet, trying to rub away the throbbing. Steel smiled when she saw moisture in his eyes.

Steel and Fleet took positions directly in front of Rock. She pressed the tip of the katana onto Rock's stomach, hard enough to make him flinch. Fleet kept the rifle aimed at Rock's head.

After a minute, Rock composed himself. He lifted his head, appraising the two of them. He glanced at the floor for a few seconds, grunted, and after taking a few deep breaths, looked up again. As if nothing had happened, Rock picked up right where he had left off.

"That's when they decided to try something different."

Rock's voice was subdued. His eyes blinked—possibly Steel speculated, in rhythm with the pounding of his head. One part of her wanted to run her katana right through him, silencing him forever, but she needed to hear the rest of the story. She wanted to find out why her parents had died, and why the rest of the world was doomed to follow. The other part of her had trouble believing Wise had been a part of all this, that he had chosen to share his story with Rock rather than her. She felt betrayed, and found it difficult to come to grips with it.

"Why did they think it was a portal?" Steel asked. "Some kind of a hole?" Pointing to it, she added, "It didn't extend through the floor. I was on the first and second levels of this building and the ceilings weren't touched. Couldn't it simply be a flat object?"

Though it was pained, a smile crept along Rock's lips. "Yeah, Wise said they ran downstairs to see how deep it went. They came back baffled. To answer your question, I think they called it a *hole* simply because it looked like one. I don't think they knew *what* to call it. Maybe that's why they began to experiment by dropping shit onto it. Like I said, when that didn't work they must have really been puzzled.

"Wise said, after thinking about it, he realized they had to try something different. He figured out that everything they put onto the object was man-made, so they decided to try something living. Wise grabbed a plant from the windowsill. He brought it back and pulled it out of its pot. Then he threw it onto the hole."

"What happened?" Fleet blurted.

Rock looked him straight in the eye. "It went through the surface. It *was* a hole after all."

Fleet looked as if he had been hit with a lightning bolt; his head jolted back a few inches, his eyes grew wide, and he mouthed the word *wow*.

Steel knew from Fleet's reaction that, just as she, he was visualizing the story as Rock told it. Though she was as enthralled by the tale as Fleet was, she kept her emotions in check.

"Weird, huh?" Rock continued. "Know what else? The plant went through no problem, but the dirt stayed on the surface. Wise said they were all spooked while looking at the dirt, wondering what in hell this thing was. Can you guys picture them around the hole imagining what would happen next? Would the plant come flying back out? If it did, would it be changed? Would Holden order one of them to strip naked and then jump into it?"

Rock paused and grimaced while rubbing the back of his head before continuing with his story.

"Wise said it felt like hours, but they waited only a short time for something to happen. When nothing did, Holden announced she was going to find a cat, and then she bolted from the room to the stairway. While she was gone, the rest of them continued to stand around, afraid to do anything else. Wise used the time to research the author of the pamphlet—Long Elk.

"Wise found Long Elk mentioned in a newspaper article written in 1880. Long Elk was an American Indian, a member of the Goshutes tribe, and his kids murdered a local farmer named Dyer, in Spring Valley. The article detailed the murder, and it said his kids hung for the crime, but there was no further mention of Long Elk. Wise looked up the Goshutes and discovered that they were heavily involved in some type of bizarre mysticism. They believed beings from other spirit worlds existed and they could call on these beings to help them out when things got particularly nasty for them. According to Wise's research, summoning them was tricky; it had to be done in a specific manner. If the Indian who called them screwed it up, it could open portals to more than one world, and there was no telling which worlds, or what would come through those portals. If that happened, it could mean the end of life as the Indians knew it.

Fleet interrupted Rock. "Wait a minute—are you trying to tell us that the reason the world is the way it is, is because of some old Indian superstition?"

"Yeah, I am."

Steel took a moment to absorb Rock's revelation. It sounded ridiculous; ancient Indians, a summoning, some kind of otherworldly beings—but her gut told her otherwise. She turned to the hole and glimpsed into its blackness. Visions of the first day of the gray rain and the madness that resulted played in her mind. She lost her parents, her very way of life, because some government assholes were looking into a supernatural way to win wars. She closed her eyes and squeezed her hands into fists. Though she had the answer she longed for, there was no satisfaction in it. There was an ache in her chest, a hollowness. They were up against beings from another world. She, and everyone in the shelter had been fighting a battle they couldn't win. They'd never even had a chance.

"Can I finish the story now?" Rock asked.

With all the fight in her drained, Steel nodded.

"Wise couldn't find much more on Long Elk or the Goshutes. He got tired of waiting for Holden to return, so he decided to go over the translation again to see if it had any clue as to what purpose this hole served, searching for some kind of explanation. When he came to one particular passage, he got excited and called a coworker over to discuss it. He wound up reading the passage out loud to the guy. And, that, was the beginning of the end. Wise told me he figured out afterward the pamphlet they had from Long Elk contained various summonings, and the computer translated them as one. The first time he read from it, the hole appeared from one of those worlds. The second time, he tapped into a different world.

"Wise said the moment he finished reading, every window on the floor shattered, and then the hole exploded. Like a geyser, only made up of what seemed to be dense gray smoke instead of water. It was as solid as a column of steel. He said the column rose so fast they didn't even see it break through the ceiling. But, get this: no debris rained down on them. Wise said it penetrated the roof like a laser, cutting through so clean you couldn't see a space between the column and the ceiling. And, as strange as all of this was, he said what was even weirder was they never heard a sound, from either the explosion or the column plowing through the ceiling. All they heard were each other's gasps or screaming.

"When they realized they weren't going to die, they calmed down enough to approach the column and study it. It shimmered, he said, looking like heat waves rising up from a stove. And, between those waves, they all could have sworn that they'd seen faces floating around. The faces—spectral faces, he called them—rose up the pillar with the waves. There had been so many of them that they couldn't be counted."

A shiver ran through Steel, and she turned toward Fleet. She was not surprised to see him looking back at her, his face pale, the rifle shaking in his hands.

She turned back to Rock, waiting to hear more. When she faced him, an odd feeling made her neck go stiff. Something wasn't right. She looked at Fleet again, wondering if he felt it, but Fleet had already turned back to Rock, waiting for him to continue, not showing any signs of being disturbed. She relaxed a bit, chalking the odd feeling up to Rock's story.

For his part, Rock seemed amused by their reactions. He rubbed the back of his head again and continued with his story. "About then, Captain Holden came running back into the room, but stopped short when she saw the column. And, yes, she did have a cat in her hands. Dropping the cat to the floor, she told them that they should follow her outside. All too happy to leave the building, they scrambled down the stairway and into the street. When they crossed to the other side, they stopped and looked up to the roof. That's when the panic really set in.

"The column reached high into the clouds. At its top, it seemed to hit an invisible ceiling. It mushroomed out, spreading slowly in all directions. Wise said it reminded him of an atomic bomb cloud. For days it lingered over the building, then—"

Rock stopped speaking. A smile spread over his face.

Steel tilted her head slightly to the side. *Why did he stop talking*? Rock nodded his head, and she realized she had screwed up.

As the wire slipped around her neck, Steel cursed her own stupidity.

# CHAPTER TEN

As Steel's head reared back, Fleet had to decide whether to keep the rifle trained on Rock or confront whoever had grabbed her. Instinct drove him, and he pivoted the gun toward Steel. When he saw her assailant, he froze. Rock took advantage of his hesitation, and pulled the rifle from Fleet's grasp. Still too shocked to move, Fleet never saw the butt of the weapon speeding to the side of his head.

Fleet lay on the floor, stars floating in and out of his vision. He shook his head a few times to chase them away, and when he was able to concentrate, he saw Steel lying next to him. She struggled to breathe and he reached for her. When their eyes met, he expected to see fury burning in hers—instead, they were distant; dull.

Steel lay on her back with her arms by her side and her legs stretched out to their fullest. Her cheeks puffed in and out as she inhaled as much air as her windpipe would allow. Fleet took note of how measured her actions were. If it were him, he would have grasped his neck with both hands and thrashed like a madman. But, Steel remained calm, regulating her breathing until she could get it back to normal. Fleet's admiration for her increased—she was the toughest person he had ever met. He looked up at her assailant. Whisper wore a crooked smile as she peered at Steel. In Whisper's hand was a wire with wooden handles attached to each end.

*A garrote! She could have killed Steel with that thing!*

Fleet's gaze locked on Whisper. What was her connection to all of this? How could she hurt Steel after all Steel had done for her? His stomach churned with the thought of her betrayal.

"Why?" he muttered aloud standing.

"I wanted out."

"You—you can talk?" Fleet stammered. Behind him came a throaty laugh.

"Hell, yeah, she can talk."

Whisper walked around Fleet and took a position beside Rock. The rifle in Rock's hands pointed at Steel's head as he addressed Fleet.

"Whisper doesn't say all that much, but when she has something to say, she manages to get it out just fine. You know, we spent a lot of time together these last couple of weeks. We got real close. And, now, she's convinced, like I am, that there are others out there who've managed not only to survive, but to thrive. There are people in the world who can help us, feed us, and maybe have an antidote for the madness when we turn. We're going to find them. If you had felt the same way," he continued, turning to Steel and spitting the words with venom, "we wouldn't be where we are now. Would we?"

Steel continued to catch her breath, ignoring him.

Rock turned to Whisper. "Light the candles and set them up on the desks. It's getting dark, and I want to be able to see what happens next."

Whisper nodded and walked over to one of the far desks surrounding the hole. She opened a drawer and removed a number of tall white candles, placing them on top of the desk. She lit them one by one, and placed most of them on the desks circling the hole. She put the rest on the floor in a pattern that surrounded the four of them. When she finished, Rock nodded toward Steel's katana, and Whisper went to fetch it.

"Place the tip against the back of Fleet's neck. Drive it in, but only enough to draw blood." Rock leaned forward and placed the end of the barrel against Steel's forehead. "And, Fleet, don't think about running or I'll blow her head off."

Fleet had no choice. Whisper circled behind him and, seconds later, pricked the back of his neck. His body tensed and he yelped. Whisper held the katana in place.

"Now, Steel," Rock commanded, "I want you to remove your clothes."

"What?" she asked hoarsely. "What did you say?"

Instead of answering, Rock nodded toward Whisper, who pushed the tip of the katana a little deeper into Fleet's neck. Fleet screamed from the pain and almost collapsed, but Whisper pulled the sword back a bit and he remained on his feet.

Rock answered, sarcasm dripping from his voice. "Both Fleet and I have seen you naked, Steel—and I confess to enjoying the sight—but Whisper hasn't. From what I've come to know of her, I'm sure she will be as appreciative of your body as Fleet and I were. Now, take off your clothes!" Rock pulled the gun from her forehead and stepped back.

With her head bowed, Steel rose from the floor. She removed her clothes and placed them in a small pile. Fleet noted how dirty and ragged they were. Funny how he never noticed that while she was wearing them. When she finished, Steel lifted her head, and stared straight ahead. She made no attempt to cover herself. Fleet wasn't surprised. She looked defiant, fists balled tight and eyes fierce.

"Now," Rock demanded, "stand on that." He nodded to the desk closest to him.

"No!" Fleet shouted.

For his outburst, Fleet was rewarded with a jab into the back of his neck with a sideways slice. Warm blood flowed down his back. The pain was too much. He groaned and dropped to his knees, the tip of the katana moving along with him.

Spit flew from Rock's mouth as he screamed, "The next time, she'll run it through you, so shut the hell up!" Rock turned back to Steel. "Get up on that desk now or Whisper will kill him right where he's kneeling."

Steel walked to the desk, climbed, and stood atop it. The fury in her eyes had not abated, and Fleet questioned whether she knew what Rock had planned for her.

Rock approached Steel with the rifle pointed at her stomach. He stopped short of the desk. "Turn around, Steel!"

Again, Steel obeyed.

Fleet lowered his head into his hands and sobbed loudly. Seconds later, he lifted his head. Steel was gone, and Rock was standing at the desk, looking into the hole.

# CHAPTER ELEVEN

Fleet didn't know how late it was, but he was sure it was hours after sunset. The burning rains were falling particularly hard this evening: he could hear it slapping against the windows, and puddles formed on the floor beneath broken glass. In a dry spot with his back to the wall, the monotonous sound of the rain proved to be calming. He lifted his head—the rain wasn't pouring in through the hole in the ceiling. Whatever that thing was on the floor, it had power. Thinking of the hole brought Steel to mind. He shivered and shook his head in an attempt to block out what had happened to her. Now wasn't the time to go there—he wasn't ready to accept her fate.

Fleet caught the shadow dance of candles on the walls. After watching for a few moments, he recalled Rock's story and imagined the shadows to be the flickering profiles of angry Indians or otherworldly beings waiting for our world to die so they could take it over. He diverted his gaze to the circle of desks around the hole. Rock and Whisper sat side by side, facing him. Rock relaxed with the rifle across his lap and Whisper studied the katana. Both may have been bored—probably disappointed that Steel hadn't resurrected from the hole.

Fleet wasn't sure why they hadn't tied him up. *Maybe, they didn't have any rope?* It was piss-poor planning on Rock's part, if it were the case. Not that it mattered much; they had a pretty good eye on him, and he wasn't in any position to get the jump on them.

"I have no issue with you, Fleet, never have," Rock said. "Steel was my problem. In the morning, you can go back to the shelter and take care of Cookie and Daisy. Hell, you can even come along with us if you want. But, I'm not going to wait for you to get them and return. What do you say?"

When Rock mentioned the names of the two girls, Fleet's eyes went wide. With everything that had happened, he had forgotten all about them and hoped they were okay. He resolved to make his way back to the shelter as soon as possible. He mulled over Rock's offer and considered the variables. All the scenarios in his head resulted in the same conclusion—that he would never feel safe traveling with Rock and Whisper. Rock was a murderer for what he had done to Steel. Whisper was a wild card, though. Fleet didn't know her well enough to understand what role she had played in all of this. Either Rock had brainwashed her into believing that there was a better life for them out there or she had her own purpose in standing by Rock's side. So far, all her actions had put her squarely in Rock's corner.

"I'm going to head back to the shelter in the morning," Fleet told Rock.

Rock smiled. "I figured you would. You and Steel are a lot alike. You share her trait for loyalty but lucky for you, you don't have her knack for arrogance. Like I said, you're free to go in the morning. I recommend you get some sleep. Whisper and I will be taking turns watching over the hole so there will always be one of us awake. I wouldn't attempt anything if I were you. Just because I said I would let you go doesn't mean I won't kill you if you try something stupid."

Fleet almost laughed out loud. Every option he had except for waiting until morning would prove to be stupid. Instead, he nodded and slid down the wall until he was sitting on his butt. From there, he sprawled onto the floor and rolled onto his left side, resigned to getting some rest. Depressed and tired, Fleet was asleep in a matter of minutes.

# CHAPTER TWELVE

Whisper was the first to wake. The candle on her desk had fallen over and singed her shirt. A sharp pain on her arm and the smell of smoke had her sitting upright. After extinguishing the flame, she was aware of a low vibration in the room. She scanned the area and saw nothing unusual. Turning her gaze toward the hole, she stared at it for a few seconds before she reached over and shook Rock.

"Wha-what?" he muttered. "Shit, I'm sorry. I must have dozed off." He rose and stood in front of the desk. Shaking the sleep from his head, he asked her, "Is it Fleet? Did he leave?"

Whisper shook her head. She pointed to the hole.

When he heard his name, Fleet's eyes flew open and he sprang from the floor. He looked around the room but saw nothing familiar. It took a few seconds for the fog to dissipate, and when it did, he breathed heavily and ran his fingers through his hair. As his situation came back into focus, a vision of Rock with a rifle pointed at him popped into his head. Fleet scrambled against the wall. His pulse slowed after he noticed Rock and Whisper at the desk, their backs turned to him.

Looking out the windows, Fleet saw that the sky was still dark, though the burning rain had reduced to a drizzle. Morning wasn't too far off. If he were true to his word, Rock would let him leave without harm. Turning his attention to Rock and Whisper, he was curious as to why they were ignoring him. Maybe now was a good time to head to the stairway, wait below for the rains to stop, and then head back to the shelter. The decision was made for him when Rock spun around and asked him to join them.

Rock hadn't pointed the rifle at him—the barrel was trained on the hole. When Fleet reached the desk, he looked down.

The surface of the hole was rippling.

Small pockets of dark matter bubbled in its center. One after another, they burst, forming waves that spread out evenly in all directions. When the waves broke against the perimeter of the hole, the floor vibrated and the desks rattled.

*What's causing those air bubbles to rise to the surface?*

Though he wasn't sure what was happening, his skin crawled.

The bubbles stopped rising and the surface turned flat. The vibration of the floor ceased and the desks were still. His eyes glued to the hole, Fleet waited. The air turned heavy, pressure built in his sinuses and his ears plugged. His heartbeat accelerated, and he shivered.

Fleet's eyes grew wide when he became aware that he was leaning toward the hole. He struggled to regain control and managed to pull back, but it wasn't far enough to spare him when the center of the hole erupted.

He was blown across the room.

Fleet hit the wall hard and spilled to the floor in a heap. His shoulder and right side took the brunt of the impact. While he was in pain, he didn't think he had broken any bones. He lay there, breathing hard, and waited for the hurt to subside. After a few moments, he sat up, leaned against the wall, and gazed around him. He blinked a few times in the hope that what he was seeing would prove to be an illusion. The entire room was awash in black holes, ranging from inches to a couple of feet in diameter. They were strewn randomly, but with a few exceptions, there was enough space to walk between them.

Fleet's eyes roamed the room until he saw Rock and Whisper crumpled on the floor. They were alive but their movements were hesitant. While Fleet questioned his reasoning, he was relieved that they hadn't been killed from the blast. His relief turned to concern when he saw that one of Whisper's arms was missing. Looking closer, he saw he was mistaken—her arm dangled in one of the holes. Everything below her elbow had been swallowed.

With a groan, Whisper rolled onto her back and eased her arm out of the hole. She and Rock crawled toward Fleet and leaned against the wall, beside him. Rock had managed to cling to his rifle, but the katana ended up resting against the wall, a few feet away from Whisper.

Something was rising from behind the desks. When it reached a foot above the desktop, recognition slammed Fleet's head back against the wall. He struggled to get the attention of the other two. The best he could manage was a barely audible, "L-look!"

He tried again with the same results.

Fleet pointed to the desk, his hand trembling. He swallowed and attempted to warn them once more. When he got the words out, his shout was so loud it echoed against the walls. "*Look!*"

Rock and Whisper's eyes followed his outstretched arm. When they saw what was behind the desk, Rock shouted, "*Holy shit!*" Their hands and heels scuffed against the floorboards in an attempt to scramble away. With their backs against the wall, there was nowhere to go.

Steel ascended gracefully from behind the desk, as if she had been called to heaven by angels. However, when she came into full view, Fleet knew the term *angel* would have been a blasphemy. While there was no doubt whose face he was staring at, it was *off* somehow—crooked and devoid of life. Pasted onto the head of a monster was Steel's visage. It was an abstract—a mask made of flesh. The edges around it were ragged, as if cut by a toddler with garden shears. Though it retained her features and color, the surrounding flesh, including the skull, was fluorescent orange. The abomination was hairless but not bald—atop its head sat a nest of snakes. Five serpents, extending a foot or more, writhed in random patterns above its head. At the tip of each snake were lips—fleshy and bright pink. The lips snapped at the air like baby birds reaching for their next meal. Fleet could hear their chatter from where he sat. He shuddered—there had to be teeth in those lips to make such a noise.

As the orange monstrosity continued to rise from behind the desk, the three cowered against the wall. Rock and Whisper alternated between whimpers and loud cries, but Fleet remained silent, mesmerized by the sight.

After it had attained its full height, the creature stepped onto the desk. It stood about eight feet tall and was wide as a doorway. The rest of its body was the same fluorescent orange as its head. Its build, like nothing Fleet had ever seen, reminded him of a balloon figure a magician would make for little kids at a birthday party. It had tubular-shaped arms and legs, and more of those snake-like appendages writhed in place of fingers and toes. A large pair of cone-shaped breasts with nipples as wide and long as Fleet's little finger jutted from its chest. Standing rigid on the desk, it stared slightly above them, as if they weren't there.

Fleet's shoulders slumped and he lowered his head—whatever this was, this beast might have once been Steel.

He turned to the others. "Hey, guys—now might be a good time to get out of here." When neither responded, Fleet spoke louder and with more urgency. "Rock, Whisper, look at me!" Both turned toward him, their eyes wide. "Rock, get your rifle ready in case it comes after us. Whisper, pick up that katana."

It took a few seconds for Rock to snap out of his daze. He pulled the rifle up to his chest and pointed the barrel toward the creature on the desk. Whisper was still staring at Fleet, her eyes wide, unfocused. Rock turned to her, "Come on, bitch, snap out of it! Pick up the damn sword!"

Fleet wasn't sure if it was Rock's shout or being called a bitch that broke Whisper from her trance. She turned from Fleet and reached for the katana. She was calm and deliberate as she lifted the weapon from the floor. Her eyes traveled the length of the blade, inspecting it for damage. Satisfied there was none, she swung the sword in arcs, cutting the air in front of her as she checked its balance. Fleet assumed it must have met her expectations as she then grasped its handle with both hands and stood. She stared ahead, holding the katana steady, the tip pointed at the abomination. Fleet shook his head at her transformation—he found himself questioning her relationship with Rock once more.

In the wake of Whisper's newfound bravado, Fleet rose from the floor while keeping his eyes on the monster. Rock, too, stood and asked, "What do you think we should do?"

Fleet's response was quick. "Judging by the light, the burning rain should be over by now."

Rock nodded while Whisper maintained her stance. "Whisper," Fleet called, "we're getting out of here. You coming?" When there was no answer, he turned to her. Whisper's face was tight, her eyes narrow and her lips curled. Was she deep in thought, working something out in her head? After he called her name a few more times, Whisper turned to him and nodded. With Fleet in the lead, the three of them retreated to the stairway.

They skirted the holes on the floor, standing as close to each other as space allowed. Fleet dreaded turning his back on the creature, but there were too many holes, and he had to pay attention. Though it slowed them down—and in a few cases it caused them to run into each other—he frequently glanced back as they made their way to the staircase. So far, the beast hadn't moved since having stepped onto the desk, and it continued staring at the wall.

At the halfway point, Fleet looked back. He froze. Did he see movement? He let Rock and Whisper pass him and then turned to face the monster. Fleet looked for signs of awareness, something that would have made him think it moved. Seeing nothing, he focused on its face. Steel's face. Was she somehow trapped in that body? He hoped not—he would rather have seen her dead and away from all the pain and suffering that came with this new world. But, if she were somehow trapped inside that—

The creature snapped its head toward him.

Fleet's crotch dampened and he stumbled back a step. He knew he should run, but he couldn't look away. The beast's stare burned through him. In that moment, he knew—the mask was all that was left of Steel.

With its eyes on Fleet, the creature bent its legs into a crouching position. It jumped, and aimed toward the center of a large hole on the floor in front of the desks. Before its feet made contact with the hole, two large florescent orange hands broke the surface and connected with the bottom of the creature's feet. They served as a platform, easily supporting its weight and preventing it from sinking. In a path between Fleet and the creature, more hands popped up out of the holes that dotted the floor. The hands were stationary, palms up, waiting to assist their summoner in reaching its prey. Fleet knew he should be running, but he couldn't make himself move. He couldn't pull his eyes away from the monstrosity and all those orange hands.

# CHAPTER THIRTEEN

"**F**LEET!"

The hold on Fleet broke when he heard his name called. It wasn't so much his name that brought him back—it was the sound of the voice. He had thought it Steel's, and his heart leapt. But, that didn't make sense. Steel, or what used to be Steel was headed toward him on orange hands. The voice had come from behind him, but when he turned to seek its source, there was no one there. Farther on, Rock and Whisper glanced at him as they approached the stairway. While Rock did not look in Fleet's direction as he slipped past the door, Whisper paused, waiting. "Hurry!" she shouted.

Fleet sprinted toward them, dodging the many holes along the way. When Whisper saw he was following, she scrambled through; the tip of the katana trailed her through the door and Fleet watched it disappear. As he approached the door, he reached out, wrapped one hand around the frame, and then swung himself around to glide through it. He pulled the door shut and spun the wheel, praying to God a bolt would engage to lock it. The wheel turned easily in his hands, and when it stopped, he made his way down the poorly lit staircase, avoiding the holes scattered along the steps. He listened for the sound of the door opening, or of its destruction. Hearing neither, he slowed, concentrating on the placement of the holes on the stairs. They were larger than the ones closer to the door, and though he still had space to maneuver around them, there wasn't much room to spare. When he had made it past the second floor, he stopped dead in his tracks, shaking his head at the sight before him. It was Whisper, or at least a portion of Whisper—she had fallen into one of the holes on the stairway. He could only see her back, from her waist up. He choked back a sob. *She'd been cut in half!*

Fleet screamed when she turned to look at him.

Whisper grunted and motioned with her head for him to come over and help her. He exhaled—she was still alive! He closed the gap between them and circled in front of her. The katana lay across the width of the hole and Whisper's bloody hands gripped the blade. Fully extended, her arms shook from the strain of supporting her body.

Fleet leaned over and wrapped his arms below her breasts. He planted his feet, bent his knees, and pulled with all his strength. He didn't know what to expect. Whisper rose a foot, and relief washed over him—but then a violent tug brought her back down. She held the katana tighter, the blood from her hands running faster.

"Something's got me!" she cried.

Fleet adjusted his grip. He stooped low, worried that he might lose his balance. Visions of both of them plunging into the hole played in his head. Whisper shook so much that he feared her arms would give out. He had to calm her down if they were going to get out of this.

"Whisper, I'm going to try this again. You've got to loosen the hold it's got on you. When I count to three, I want you to kick your legs and throw whatever's got you off balance. Can you do that?"

With her eyes closed tight from the pain, Whisper nodded.

Fleet encouraged her. "Good. Now here we go. One. Two. *Three!*"

Fleet pulled. Sharp pain flared in his lower back, and his neck felt like it was on fire. Whisper did her part—he could tell by the way her torso rocked that she was kicking her legs. Fleet kept pulling, screaming through gnashed teeth until he was positive the muscles in his arms were going to burst.

The next thing Fleet knew, he was falling.

His lower back took the brunt of the fall, and while he was in pain, he didn't think any bones were broken. He lay still, eyes closed and took deep breaths before checking the rest of his body. There was an ache in his arms, but they moved freely. His legs obeyed his commands and he could turn his neck without grimacing, but there was an odd sensation on his stomach. Opening his eyes, he saw a mop of hair resting against his chest. *Whisper!* Stretching his arms and legs to loosen them, he gently moved her aside. When he stood and saw her condition, he stiffened and took a step backward. He shook his head as his gaze traveled from Whisper's feet to her head. When their eyes met, hers were focused on him. There was the hint of a smile on her lips, and her eyes were soft with gratitude. *She doesn't know what had happened to her.* He smiled back, but he couldn't help himself—his eyes went back to her lower body.

She had been wearing pants when they were running from the monster. She still had them on, but below her crotch, the legs of her pants were missing, as if they'd dissolved. Fleet couldn't see any loose threads or torn fabric—only a smooth hem. While her legs were still attached and whole, they had undergone a change: now they were fluorescent orange. Fleet was thankful there weren't snakes weaving around where toes should have been.

Fleet started to ask Whisper if she were okay, but when she saw his expression, she didn't give him the time to ask. She sat up, peering at her legs. Gasping, she started kicking, as if she could shake them off like a pair of old boots. The kicking was fruitless. She stared at her legs for a few moments, and then leaned forward and touched them. Seconds later, the tension melted from her features. She stood, and then walked a few paces around the hole.

"They feel okay, Fleet—normal in fact. Except for the color, there doesn't seem to be anything else wrong with them."

Fleet swallowed. "Are you sure?"

She took a few more steps. "Yeah."

"Then let's get the hell out of here."

Whisper picked up the katana and led the way down to the first floor. Fleet followed closely behind. Inappropriate thoughts dogged him. *She wouldn't be tough to find at the beach... I wonder how far up that color goes.* He forced his mind out of the gutter and concentrated on their escape.

When they reached the first floor, Whisper stopped short, and Fleet ran into her. She stumbled but recovered quickly. After she regained her balance, Fleet heard her swear. Whisper swung the katana up, pointing it ahead of them. Fleet went to her side and checked the floor. Rock sat on the long counter, nestled between two holes, his rifle pointed in their direction.

Rock's gaze fixed on Whisper's legs. "I guess there's no need to ask you guys what took you so long."

Fleet never got the chance to reply.

Large chunks of wood and shattered glass from the entrance of the building exploded into the air. Rock jumped off the desk without looking behind and rushed to join Fleet and Whisper at the bottom of the stairs. The three of them stood side by side, staring at the entrance doors. The top halves of the doors were smashed to pieces. A few shards of glass jutted from the frames, but their hold must have been tenuous, as they heard a tinkle every few seconds. The bottom portions of the door were intact but not aligned, the panes crisscrossed with cracks.

The building turned quiet. Nobody moved—all eyes were locked on the entrance door. They waited. Seconds passed, then minutes. Still, nothing happened. Beside him, Whisper and Rock stood stiff, their knuckles white from gripping their weapons. Attuned to the silence, Fleet picked up small noises: a creak of the floorboards, Rock swallowing, a small hiss as Whisper exhaled through her nose. He could have sworn he heard the beating of his own heart.

The sound was deafening as the remainder of the twin doors exploded.

More glass and wood fragments flew through the air. The trio turned from the assault, covering their heads with their arms until the noise died down. When they turned back, the creature stood in the doorway, its head moving from side to side, in a deliberate, studious motion. The snakes on its head and limbs darting about as if sniffing the air, like a wolf honing in on its prey. When one of the snakes spotted Fleet, the rest turned in his direction.

The beast stepped forward but stopped short—its body was bigger than the opening of the metal detector. After studying the obstruction, it reached out with both hands and grabbed the columns. The beams buckled in its grip, and it pushed them aside as if they were cardboard. The monster swiveled its gaze back to the stairway and advanced toward the counter.

It was coming for them.

"Split up!" Fleet shouted, bolting to his left. He saw Rock take off to the right, but Whisper stood her ground.

"Whisper, get the hell out of there!"

Without a word, Whisper raised the katana extended in front of her, arched her back and bent her knees slightly.

*Oh my God,* thought Fleet, *she's going to take it on!* The creature moved to within a few feet of the long counter and paused, and focused on Whisper. It leapt.

The abomination flew up, almost touching the ceiling, but came down only a few feet in front of the counter, its legs compressing slightly when it landed, like springs. *Why didn't it leap far enough to reach Whisper? Maybe it can jump high or jump a great height, but not so for distance. Is that because of its bulk?*

When the monster had approached them upstairs, it had leapt off the desk and the orange hands had supported it. *Is it so heavy it can't move very fast without those hands? Are they pushing it along?*

The creature stood still and closed its eyes. Moments later, the holes in the floor between Whisper and the beast erupted with outstretched orange hands.

"Whisper," Fleet yelled. "Those hands are moving it along, giving it speed. Use the sword!"

Whisper turned to him, eyebrows raised and head cocked to one side. Fleet nodded, urging her on. Her face tightened, but then her eyes widened. She stepped to the nearest hole and swung the katana, slicing the hand above the hole clean off. It fell into the blackness. The creature did not make a move toward her.

Fleet's heart beat faster as she moved to other holes, cutting off more hands. Whisper backtracked, and stood by the stairway, not risking approaching the monster any closer.

Fleet turned to the beast. Its eyes followed the path of

holes between itself and its prey. It moved forward, its left leg descended into a hole, and an orange hand reached up to support it. The creature did the same with its right leg. When it had crossed half the distance to Whisper, it halted—Whisper had lopped off all of the hands in the remaining holes, and none rose to replace them. Having no choice, the creature sidestepped the next hole, placing its legs onto solid ground. It remained motionless for a few seconds, then, it took a tentative step toward Whisper.

Whisper assumed a combat position, holding the katana high and back over her right shoulder.

Fleet watched from the sidelines, trembling, unable to make a move as the scene played out before him. Instead of continuing to advance, the creature bent its legs and jumped—and Fleet had no doubt that it intended to land *on* Whisper this time.

Whisper's eyes had never left the creature, the muscles in her arms tensing as it came closer. She swung the katana, the arc of the sword true, slicing through the air like lightning. Unless God intervened, Fleet knew it would be her last act— the speed of the creature and its bulk guaranteed that it would crush her to death.

As Fleet had assumed, God remained a reclusive observer.

The katana entered its right leg below the knee, severing it cleanly. The shin sailed over several holes, landing on the floor with a soft thud. But, the amputation slowed the momentum of the katana, changing its trajectory. When the weapon cut through the left leg, the blade turned sideways and barely broke the creature's skin.

Whisper never had a chance to see the results of her blow. She grimaced just before the creature landed, its leg struck her midsection, slamming her to the floor. The katana flew from her grip as her head swung in Fleet's direction, her eyes wide with terror. Instinctively he reached to her, but in an instant, she was buried beneath an orange mountain of flesh.

Whisper's chest cavity burst, her internal organs exploding from beneath the beast. Piles of viscera littered the floor. Gray matter soon mixed with the blood, flowing into the surrounding holes. Only Whisper's orange legs were untouched. They stuck out from under the creature as if they were extensions of its body.

Bright orange liquid drained from its severed leg, mingling with Whisper's blood in a puddle.

Fleet bent over, but with nothing in his stomach, he dry-heaved. He straightened and turned to the monster. It was moving, looking at the holes, hunting for a path toward Fleet. Fleet had only seconds to flee, or, maybe, enough time to fight. When he spied the katana lying on the floor, he made his decision.

Fleet ran toward the katana, keeping his balance while dodging the holes in his way. He stopped in front of a large hole, went to one knee, and reached for the weapon. When his fingers wrapped around the handle, he charged.

Their eyes locked.

The snakes dancing around the creature's head slowed their frenetic weaving, turning as one, to Fleet, lined up and hovering. The snakes on its hands and remaining foot followed suit.

*They're standing at attention—soldiers awaiting orders.*

The triangles atop the snakes snapped. Their angry clicking stabbed Fleet's ears like miniature knives. He concentrated on the monster's eyes hoping, they would telegraph movement.

Katana in hand, Fleet stood above the creature. It stared at Fleet, head moving slightly left, then right. After a few seconds, its expression changed; the eye's narrowed, and the corners of its mouth sunk.

Fleet maintained eye contact, leaning toward the beast, trying to make sense of its expression. When the eyes widened and the corners of its mouth lifted, he understood what was happening. Fleet returned the smile. He saw a look of recognition on the creature's face. The longer Fleet stared, the more he knew he was looking into Steel's eyes.

Now was the time to strike, but Fleet couldn't do it. It wasn't Steel's fault she was trapped in that hulk of a body. Tears streamed from his eyes and he fell to his knees. "Oh, Steel, I—I don't know what to do."

Steel stared at Fleet for a few more seconds and then turned away. She crawled to a large nearby hole, reaching out with her arm tubes. Contorting the limbs to make wrists, she gripped the lip of the hole, and started pulling her body into it.

The snakes came alive. Mouths snapping erratically, their lips opened and closed like locomotive pistons. They dove at her, chewing on her flesh. One by one, they attacked and pulled back—spitting out flesh and returning for more.

Despite the assault, Steel inched further. Whisper's body, still pinned beneath her, was dragged along, leaving a red snail trail. She continued forward until her neck crossed the perimeter of the hole and her head hovered above the opening, and then she stopped.

Steel turned, facing Fleet. Her eyes bored into his.

She nodded.

Fleet understood. There was no other way to release her from that prison. With teary eyes, he returned the nod.

The snakes chewing on Steel stopped their attack. They darted toward Fleet, snapping at the air, but Fleet was out of their reach.

The katana closed that gap.

Fleet hacked away at the snakes until there was none left. When the last of them landed on the floor, he let the sword drop to his side. He moved until he stood beside Steel, and gazed down on her. She looked up at him, eyes pleading to free her from her nightmare.

Fleet gripped the katana with both hands and raised it high above his head. He looked up and silently asked God for forgiveness. After a deep breath, he lowered his head. There was movement near a hole in front of him.

Fleet froze.

He had totally forgotten about Rock, who stood ten feet away, facing them.

Fleet needed a moment to think. If he acknowledged Rock's presence, he knew Steel would change her mind; her hatred of Rock so intense, she'd find the strength to rise and kill him. Fleet might never have this chance to put her out of her misery.

Fleet turned to Steel and nodded to her once more. His old friend nodded back. She lowered her head, exposing her neck.

Fleet brought the katana down. He felt no resistance until the blade hit the side of the hole. He blinked. He couldn't believe it was over so quickly. He imagined her head tumbling forever in a dark well of emptiness.

Bright orange fluid trickled from the stump. Most of the blood spilled into the hole, but some puddled onto the floor. Fleet stared at the monster's body.

*No, this thing, this thing wasn't Steel.*

The body exploded.

The force of the blast knocked Fleet to the floor. He landed on his ass, covered in orange fluid and chunks of flesh.

*What the hell just happened?*

Fleet lifted his head. Rock was holding the rifle high with the butt against his shoulder, the barrel aimed toward the remnants of the monster.

"Wow!" Rock beamed. "I didn't expect that!"

Fleet's voice shook. "W—what did you do that for?"

"You really have to ask? With all the crap that's been going on, I wanted to make sure that thing was dead. Who knows if it could live without a head? Besides, I heard you call it Steel, and if that thing was her, all the more reason for me to make sure the bitch wouldn't get back up."

Fleet's muscles tensed. His eyes flared. Anger swept through him until the hand holding the katana shook. He closed his eyes, and dwelled on a visual scene playing in his head. He came to a decision.

Fleet opened his eyes.

Rock swung the rifle barrel toward him. "Hey there, orange-covered man, calm down. Don't do anything stupid. I know you and Steel were friends but—aaah!" Rock grimaced in pain. Wrapped around his left leg, several snakes darted at Rock, tearing his flesh. Using the rifle butt, he tried to swat them away, but they were too fast. Rock's screams were raw and high-pitched. Dropping the rifle, he grabbed at them, but this tactic didn't fare any better. Soon his hands were as bloody as his leg. He turned to Fleet, agony etched on his face. "Help me!"

Fleet nodded. He avoided the holes separating them and made his way to Rock.

"Hurry," Rock screamed. "Quick, cut them off!"

Fleet extended the katana, and with a quick flick of his

wrist, he swung. It wasn't a clean cut—Rock's femur slowed the blade down and threw it off course—but it did the job. Below the knee, Rock's left leg slipped away from his body.

It took a few moments for the pain to register. Rock looked wide-eyed at Fleet, "What did you do?" Rock lost his balance and teetered. Fleet closed the distance between them, placing his palm against Rock's chest.

Fleet pushed.

He couldn't make out Rock's final words as he passed through the hole, but their fading shrill timbre rang in Fleet's ears.

Fleet stood over the hole for a few minutes—not out of remorse or guilt, but to make sure nothing crawled back out. Once satisfied that Rock was gone, Fleet walked away, toward the counter. He could jump over it, but with his luck, he'd land in a hole. Besides, he was too exhausted. Instead, he made his way around it. When he arrived at the front entrance, he looked out into the street and sighed. There were holes everywhere.

Using caution, he started his journey back to the shelter. He brightened at the thought of seeing Cookie and Daisy again, but then remembered that he would have to explain what had happened to Steel and Rock. There was no way he could tell them the truth, but he had plenty of time to concoct a story. First, though, he needed to find food, and somewhere to wash off all the orange blood.

In the distance, the number of holes in the landscape lessened. Fleet saw plenty of them, but there were definitely fewer, spaced farther apart. *Maybe they don't go very far. Maybe I should reconsider Rock's plan for leaving and looking for others like us.* He'd talk to Daisy and Cookie about it when he reached the shelter. Who knew? Maybe there was a better life out there for them.

Fleet walked down the street with fantasies of the three of them welcomed somewhere else. Someplace new, where there was plenty of food and a refuge from the spidlers and bashers.

Fleet made his way back home to the shelter, oblivious to the orange hands springing up from the dark holes behind him.

# STORY NOTES (THE SCUM BAR)

While not its official name, the scum bar was an actual liquor establishment located in my hometown. It was part of a Chinese restaurant located on Main Street in Goffstown, N.H., and, as its nickname implies, it was not the fanciest of drinking emporiums. It was where blue-collar workers, bikers, and metalheads imbibed cheap liquor, passible Oriental food, and the occasional hookup. It was a small bar until it relocated across the street, expanding its square footage, food menu, and adding a stage to deafen their customers with high-decibel bands. Despite the move and a change of ownership over the years, the nickname stuck. To this day, ask any local in Goffstown about the scum bar and chances are they'll have an amusing or horrifying story to tell you. The original draft of this tale had these details and more, but when I finished the story, they didn't add to the plot, so I trimmed those parts.

My original intent was to write a story that took place entirely in the scum bar, but like every story I've written, things changed. My nameless thief, who is the lead character, had no choice but to venture out into the wilds of Goffstown.

My objective with "The Scum Bar" was to write a story much like my earlier tale, "The Old Man" (The Seeds of Nightmares). I wanted to write a noir-style story without supernatural underpinnings, or at best, a hint of the supernatural. I think I succeeded. "The Scum Bar" appeared in "Tough" e-magazine, the first place I submitted it. It may be the most read out of all my short stories.

# THE SCUM BAR

In the evening, the Tavern Bar wasn't a pretty sight from the street. Inside was even worse. But this was Goffstown, and with my options limited, it was the only place where I felt comfortable having a few drinks alone.

Its redundant name was supposed to be some kind of joke; no doubt the owner had thought himself a superb wit when he named it, but it never took. Instead, the locals called it The Scum Bar. The owner didn't seem to mind the nickname as he never did anything to live the moniker down.

The Scum Bar was where people went for some serious drinking, and that was exactly what Wade was doing when I walked in.

We were both thieves, second-story men, and occasionally we called on each other for advice or help on the more difficult jobs we took on. He was tall but thin, so he could shimmy through almost any size window, a real asset in our business. He was also one of the best safecrackers I ever met. What I liked about Wade was, like me, he always passed on a score if there was a potential for violence. He would take jobs only if the marks weren't home, and he never carried a weapon. I wasn't always averse to violence, but after a few rough jobs, I put those "tough guy" days behind me.

The last time I saw Wade was about three or four weeks ago. He had a new girl on his arm and was as happy as I'd ever seen him. So why was he sitting in The Scum Bar, staring down at his drink? He was a friend, and I couldn't let this go. I slipped into the seat opposite him as I ordered two scotches from a waitress hovering close by. It took a few seconds, but he finally gazed up at me. He looked like shit. His eyes were glassy, unfocused, and the corners of his lips were dipped toward the table. I asked him what was troubling him.

"They took her," he replied in a voice that was low and trailing.

"Who took who, Wade?"

"Sullivan. Sullivan and his goons. They took Sheri."

It took me a moment, but I remembered that Sheri was the name of the girl I saw him with a few weeks ago. "Wade, back up, tell me everything from the start."

He lifted his glass and emptied it. The timing was perfect; the waitress came by and set two fresh glasses of scotch on the table.

"Run a tab, honey?" she asked. I nodded back to her. Wade wrapped his hands around the drink but he didn't bring it to his lips. Instead, he told me his story.

"Sheri and I were out in Manchester for dinner last night. When we finished it was late, and when we walked back to the car a big-ass Chrysler pulled up alongside us. Sullivan and three of his goons got out. They stepped in front of us—there was no way of getting around them."

Thomas Sullivan. He was trouble on two feet. He ran an outfit out of Haverhill, Massachusetts, known for pulling messy jobs, meaning he didn't care if anyone got hurt. His specialty was knocking off jewelry stores, though many believed he was involved in a few other high-stake robberies. What the hell did he want with a small-time guy like Wade?

"Sullivan said that I had broken into the house of a friend of his in Goffstown," Wade continued. "He said that I took twenty grand out of that house, and he wanted it back. I had no fucking idea what he was talking about. I hadn't made a big score since I'd hooked up with Sheri, and that was in Vermont."

Like me, Wade never shit where he ate. We always did our jobs outside of town, outside of New Hampshire if possible.

"I told Sullivan it wasn't me, but he didn't believe it. His goons pushed me up against a wall and they started to beat the shit out of me. He told me he was taking Sheri. I could have her back when he got the money. He gave me until tomorrow."

I felt like I had just listened to the plot of a bad movie. What the hell was going on here? It didn't add up. Why would Sullivan himself come up from Massachusetts? Why didn't he let his goons handle it? And, why did they think Wade had anything to do with the robbery? Also, kidnapping wasn't Sullivan's style. It left a witness. Then I thought about how Sullivan didn't mind getting messy.

"I don't have twenty grand to give him." Wade went on, his voice cracking. "I don't even know where to get twenty grand. What the hell am I going to do?"

I didn't have twenty grand to give Wade, and I wasn't sure I would give it to him if I had it. I began to run his story through my head, picking out details that I wanted to follow up on. That's when Eddie walked through the door.

Eddie was a sleazeball, a small-time player who picked at the bones of the simple and the elderly. He was a con artist, pulling off scams about grandkids in trouble that depleted the bank accounts of retirees. I didn't trust the son of a bitch and he knew it. I usually stayed far away from Eddie, but that didn't stop him from coming over to our booth. He nodded and then slid in next to me.

"Wade, buddy!" Eddie said. "How you doing?"

Even his voice sounded slippery to me.

"I've been looking for you, pal," Eddie continued, "I've got a job for you."

At the mention of a job, Wade looked expectantly at Eddie. "You serious? How big?"

Eddie ignored the question. "It's right up your alley, Wade. It's a house close by, on Tibbetts Hill Road, easy in and out, but there's a safe we gotta get into and I ain't good with safes."

Wade leaned over until he was no more than a foot away from Eddie's face, his eyes drilled into Eddie's. "I asked how big."

For a moment, Eddie fidgeted in his seat. "I'm getting this secondhand from my source, but from what he tells me, we're looking at over fifty grand."

"I'm in," Wade said without hesitation.

I had been listening patiently up to now, but I couldn't stay quiet any longer. "Wade, what in the hell's the matter with you? This smells like a setup!"

Wade turned to me, his brow furrowed. "What do you mean?"

"This whole thing seems too neat," I explained to him. "Your girl gets kidnapped, they demand a ransom of twenty grand—which you don't have—and then this guy comes in offering you a job that will pay it off. You're being played."

It didn't take long for Eddie to get back in character. "Hey, wait," he retorted, his face a mask of innocence, "I have no idea what you guys are talking about. I don't know nothing about no kidnapping and I want no part of it. Look, Wade, you want in or not? It's got to be done soon, within the hour, because the family that lives there will be coming back tonight."

Wade continued to stare hard at Eddie. "You better not be screwing with me, Eddie," he said, "I need this job bad."

Eddie smiled. "You get half: twenty-five G's. You gotta tell me now, Wade, or I'm outta here."

"This whole thing stinks, Wade," I said, trying to reason with him, "it's too pat, it's too close to home, and the timing's too tight. Come on, man, don't do it."

For a moment, I thought Wade was going to blow the job off. He shook his head and murmured something about not knowing what to do. I was wrong. He ignored me, looked at Eddie, and said, "Let's do it."

Then the two of them left The Scum Bar.

I nursed my drink for a half hour.

*I'm not my brother's keeper.*

I kept telling myself that, but it didn't make me feel any better. I motioned to the waitress and left two twenties on the table. It was too much, but I didn't want to wait for the change.

Tibbetts Hill Road was in one of the more well-to-do neighborhoods of Goffstown. It was a long road, well-paved, with streetlights every hundred yards or so, and the homes are well-spaced out. I drove over it slowly, looking for Wade's or Eddie's car. The moon was full, and while I couldn't make out every detail on the road, there was enough light for me to navigate without a problem.

It took me a long five minutes, but I finally spotted Wade's white Ford Taurus parked in a long line of cars on the right side of the road. Someone was having a party. Could this be dumb luck, or was it part of the setup? If the party was staged, someone went through an awful lot to make sure this job got pulled off without any trouble. The source Eddie mentioned might be the neighbor of the house they were hitting. If that were the case, fifty grand cut three ways didn't leave enough for Wade to pay off Sullivan.

I reached into my glove box and took out a pair of latex gloves, slipping them on as I got out of my car. Sticking close to the line of parked vehicles, I walked up the street, passing the party. The music was loud and there were several people behind the house with drinks in their hands. I could hear an occasional raucous guffaw over the music. The house next door to the party was a good forty feet away. It was a gambrel with a two-car garage—no lights on. Three-foot-high hedges surrounded the property and gave it some natural cover. A nearby streetlight provided enough illumination for me to make my way around the grounds without fumbling blindly.

I went to the far side of the house where the garage was located and slipped in through the hedges until I was against the wall.

The side of the garage had no windows, so I was going to have to look inside through the overhead doors in the front. Poking my head around the corner, the first thing I did was look up. A motion detector was nestled in the roof's peak. I searched around and found a child's pull toy lying on the ground. I grabbed it and carefully tossed it in front of the garage. The lights on the motion detector didn't come on.

It was a bad sign but I shrugged it off. I turned the corner and stood in front of the garage. I looked inside through one of the small rectangular windows in the door. A chill went up my spine.

There were two cars parked in the garage. Those had to be the owner's.

I'm not a praying man, but I found myself asking God to give me a sign that I was at the wrong house. My prayer was answered, but not in the way I had hoped. A flashlight beam swept across the front windows of the house.

I ducked back to the side of the garage and then rushed to the rear. Keeping low and staying tight against the foundation, I walked hunched-over, following the back of the house until I came to the opposite sidewall. I crept toward the closest window and peered inside. Cringing, and on the verge of vomiting, I turned away.

It was a kids' playroom. Laid out on the floor, side by side, were five bodies—two women, one man, and two small children. Their throats and chests covered with dark stains.

I stepped away from the window, shaking, and leaned against the wall. I needed to catch my breath, to somehow banish that bloody scene from my head. However, my mind kept going back to that playroom. Something about the adults didn't add up. Why were there three of them? Why two women and one man? Then it came to me. The odd woman must have been Sheri. If Wade was still here, he didn't know that Sheri was dead. And, as soon as he had that safe open, Wade was going to be just as dead. I had to get inside.

Retracing my steps, I came to the rear door, and assumed this was how they had entered the house. I reached for the handle and it turned easily. The door led me into the kitchen where there was just enough light for me to make my way through without bumping into anything. I walked into the living room and paused. I heard movement coming from upstairs. Footsteps? I eased my way onto the stairway and tread softly. At the top, there was sound to my immediate right. There was an open door. Standing off to its side, I peered in.

The room, well lit from the streetlight, was large and appeared to be a master bedroom. Eddie stood there with his back turned to me, facing a king-sized bed. In front of him, on the wall to his far right, was an open safe. Below the safe, with his back against the wall and his legs splayed, sat Wade on the floor. His head hung low, both of his hands clutched at his stomach. Blood pooled between his thighs.

My knees went weak and I swallowed hard. I couldn't tell if Wade was alive or not. It didn't take long for the anger to start boiling within me. It had been a long time since I had wanted to hurt someone this bad.

I rushed Eddie, curling my right hand into a fist while bringing my arm back for the swing. I grunted, wanting the bastard to know I was coming for him. Sure enough, when he heard me, he turned. My fist slammed into the side of his face so hard his feet lifted from the floor. His head bounced off the wall behind the bed. He fell hard, not moving. Satisfied that he was out, I hurried around the bed and over to Wade.

I knelt down, put one hand under his chin and lifted it gently. "Wade, buddy, can you hear me?" He was still.

Then, his chin rose off my hand and he opened his eyes into small slits. "Yeah, I can hear you."

"I'm going to get you out of here."

Wade sighed. His hands slid to his sides, exposing the handle of a knife jutting from his stomach. "You gotta get the diamonds first," he whispered. "We need them to save Sheri."

*Diamonds?*

Confused, I left Wade's side and walked over to the bed. Sure as shit, an open wooden box lay there with a handful of diamonds inside. Scattered around the box were bundles of hundred-dollar bills. I guess Eddie had been counting them when I clocked him.

"Step away from the bed, please."

A woman's voice. I turned and saw her standing in the doorway. Though I had met her only that one time, I knew it was Sheri. She was pointing a handgun with a suppressor at me.

I moved toward Wade, who sat motionless against the wall. Either he had passed out or he was dead. I said her name loudly, hoping for a reaction from him.

"Sheri, who's the extra woman downstairs?"

Wade didn't so much as flinch at the mention of her name.

"No idea," answered Sheri. "She was here visiting when Eddie and I came over earlier to take care of the family. Wrong place, wrong time I guess." She laughed.

Still no reaction from Wade.

I looked down at the floor, my anger building. "You were part of the setup from the beginning, weren't you? Dating him.

Getting him to fall in love with you."

Something stirred on the floor, at the other side of the bed. Eddie moaned, sat up and rubbed his jaw. Both our heads turned to him as he struggled to get up. He must have heard me because in a shaky voice he answered my question.

"Yeah, she was in on it from the beginning. She's one of Sullivan's girls; he picked her specifically for this job. Guy who owns this house, he's a fence, and Sullivan knew he came into a nice stash of diamonds from the West Coast." Eddie stopped for a few seconds to stretch his jaw. "Sullivan came to me because I was local, but I didn't know anything about breaking into a safe. But, I knew Wade did. We just needed a way to get him involved. Sheri was our ticket."

I looked at Sheri and then back to Eddie. "How do I fit in?"

"You don't," he replied. "I'm not even sure why the hell you're here." He turned to the bed and gathered up the cash. "Sullivan told me I could keep any cash I found, and it looks like there's at least forty grand here." He transferred the bundles from hand to hand as he counted them.

I shook my head. "You planned on Wade being your fall guy for the murders. How were you going to explain his death?"

Eddie smiled as he counted. "Not sure. Sullivan said he'd take care of it. The boys will be here in about an hour, so I'm sure he's got something in mind."

"Eddie," Sheri casually called to him.

Eddie answered offhandedly, "Yeah?" He was still counting the money.

"Sully's already figured that out."

Sheri turned the gun toward Eddie and pulled the trigger. A puff of white smoke rose from the barrel of the suppressor. Eddie fell onto the bed; the blood seeping from the wound in his head soaked the blankets and the cash.

I knew Sheri was heartless but her ruthlessness was unexpected. I had to admit though, that as I watched Eddie bleed out on the bed, I took some satisfaction in the fact that there was one less sleazeball in the world.

Turning, I faced Sheri. "Let me guess. Eddie and Wade were supposed to kill each other, probably fighting over the money."

She nodded with a smile. "And it looks like you're going to be part of the mix."

I had to think fast. I couldn't run—I wouldn't have gone more than a few steps before she shot me. So I did the only thing I could think of—I dove to the floor on my side of the bed.

Small pieces of wallboard exploded above me. I went to push myself under the bed, but I was blocked by storage boxes tucked beneath it. Sheri appeared and stood over me. Defeated, I rolled onto my back and waited.

"Nice try," she said, pointing the gun between my eyes.

She screamed.

Sheri lowered the gun, and struggled to reach around to her back with her free hand. I sprang to my feet and charged, hitting her full on, pushing her backward, onto the floor. When we landed, I heard her gasp loudly. The gun tumbled out of her hand.

I stared hard at her face as I pushed myself up off her. Sheri's eyes were wide with shock, her mouth frozen in the shape of a perfect O. I hovered over her until I was satisfied she was no longer a threat. I slipped off and then I flipped her over. Wedged deep into the small of her back was a knife. I slid over to Wade to thank him for what he had done.

Wade was dead.

There was not a lot of time to think about what had just happened or how it had happened. I needed to get the hell out of there. I stood and prepared to leave, but I hesitated at the end of the bed.

I scooped up half the diamonds out of the box and grabbed as much dry cash as I could stuff into my pockets.

Now, here I am back at The Scum Bar. The booth where Wade and I sat earlier is empty, so I slide into it. The same waitress we had comes over. I order a scotch. I slip both of the hundred-dollar bills into her apron. "If anyone asks," I tell her, "I never left this booth." She smiles, pockets the bills and says before leaving, "No problem, honey."

Sitting here with a drink, I can finally wrap my head around what happened. Though I figure I'm lucky as hell that Wade had enough life in him to stab Sheri in the back, I'm amazed at the willpower it must have taken for him to do it. I can't imagine the pain Wade felt when he learned Sheri was part of the setup. I'm confident that Sullivan couldn't have known I was there; I was never part of the plan to begin with. Sullivan's boys will find the remaining diamonds and the cash on the bed, and that should keep him satisfied. I'm also pretty sure that Sullivan doesn't give a rat's ass about Sheri. After all, he pimped her out to Wade in the first place. Sullivan will tell his boys to leave some cash on the bed and the cops will have no problem tying it all up.

Looking around this dump, I think it's time for me to go away for a while. Not for too long though, because I got those old feelings back. I want to hurt someone, and Sullivan is going to pay for what he did to Wade. In the meantime, I've decided I'm going to do what I came here to do in the first place.

I'm going to drink my scotch.

# STORY NOTES (THE THAUMATURGE)

*I* have no idea where the idea for "The Thaumaturge" came from. *I recall wanting to write a tale alluding to racism and its consequences, but I had a difficult time focusing on a metaphor to base it on. For some odd reason, the image of a medieval king wouldn't stop entering my head. I decided to go with it. The next thing I knew, I was writing a story about Roman-era war and the undead.*

*Around the same time, Phil Perron asked me to contribute a story for his magic spell and witchcraft anthology entitled* Invocations. *I had a story called "Eyes" that I had been working on for years that would have been perfect for* Invocations, *so if he didn't care for "Eyes", I could have used this story as a backup.*

*The inclusion of a witch in "The Thaumaturge" came seamlessly to me, except I didn't know what witches were called back then. I did some research and discovered one of the terms used was thaumaturge. Though I couldn't pronounce it, I loved the imagery of the word. I used it in the story and decided to title the tale with it.*

*Phil accepted "Eyes", and "The Thaumaturge" went into the trunk.*

*Two years later, editor Sheila Shedd emailed me asking if I had a zombie story floating in the ether. She was working with Ricky Chambers on a U.K. charity anthology to benefit kids with cancer. The anthology was called* Night of the Living Cure, *and she was looking for a few U.S. writers to contribute. I had one unpublished story at the time, and, you guessed it, it was "The Thaumaturge". It fit the call perfectly, so I submitted it. Sheila read the story, and it became one of my most memorable acceptances. She emailed me back with two words: "Holy fuck!"*

# THE THAUMATURGE

The king's eyes watered as the stink washed over him. He faced five hundred men in loose rank, none of whom had bathed in days. Without a breeze, the odor permeated the air. While the smell was nauseating enough, a new one, urine, wafted from the soil. Moments earlier, the king's army had spotted their enemy marching into the sunbaked valley separating them—they were vastly outnumbered.

His realm had celebrated peace with the Black City these past twenty-five years. Until recently, there had been no signs of discord. His queen had been born into the citizenry of the Black City—her blood noble. His marriage to her, along with her annual visits to her birthplace, were instrumental in assuring peace between the two realms. However, he had noticed that for a period of time after her return from each visit, she became solemn, indifferent to her duties, never more so than after her most recent trip to the Black City.

Though she was initially reluctant, his wife had appeared to have accepted her destiny, and she had proved to be a supportive, if not overly affectionate, partner. With the exception of the time spent with her thaumaturge and their first-born son, Bekitt, she had mostly kept her own council through the years. He had loved his wife from the moment he had laid eyes on her. He had never been tempted to stray from that love or its obligations. But, now, looking over the heads of his men and into the valley, he wondered...*had his love blinded him*?

He cursed himself for his complacency. Had she learned of the Black Army's plans long ago and kept them to herself? If so, to what purpose? She loved her children, though she preferred

Bekitt over their second-born, Erin. Surely, she would not have put either of them in harm's way. He shook the thought from his mind and lowered his gaze.

Five men, the commanders of his army, stared at their king awaiting his orders. Two of them, the youngest of the commanders, were his sons. These men would relay his commands and words of encouragement to the soldiers, and then lead them into battle. Though the five were no more than a few arm lengths away, the king's voice rose so as many as possible could hear him.

"The Black Army has come to engage us in battle. They come without provocation, without terms of settlement, and without mercy. They come to strip away everything we had built in our and our ancestors' lifetimes. The Red City is a peace-loving city. We value family above all else. The Black Army shares none of our beliefs." The king's voice rose higher. "They come to wage WAR! They come to DESTROY your homes! They come to RAPE your women! They come to make your children SLAVES! But, make no mistake, above all, they are coming to kill YOU."

The king closed the distance between himself and his commanders. He walked to the first in line and proceeded to pass before each of them. "YOU are the only thing standing between who you love, what you love, and certain death. It is YOUR DUTY, to king, to country, and most of all to family—TO FIGHT! FIGHT! Strike at your enemy! Kill them before they kill you! Show them that the gods favor the hands of the righteous! Show them that the gods favor the hands of the Red Army!"

Lifting his sword high, the king thrust it into the air. His commanders mimicked his actions, and soon the entire Red Army had their arms stretched high.

"TO KING, COUNTRY, AND MOST OF ALL, FAMILY," they shouted. "FIGHT, FIGHT, FIGHT!"

Though he should have been elated at their enthusiasm, the king knew this battle would not go their way. His army had few professional soldiers. It was his own fault for leaving their ranks thin. The majority of the soldiers were farmers and merchants, all family men who were here only as a last resort to save their loved ones. His makeshift army carried swords, but the weapons were not honed properly, the men not trained in their use. A few hundred of them—the professional soldiers—wore body armor, but years of slovenly care or outright neglect made the metal vulnerable. Too many years of peace had made his men soft. Made him soft.

After conferring with the five commanders, they split the soldiers into divisions and marched into the valley to confront the Black Army. The distance between the armies was several *leuga*, and the king used the time before they engaged to position himself on a hill overlooking the valley. Surrounded by his bodyguards, he motioned his first advisor over to speak to him.

"Bring me the thaumaturge."

The first advisor's face turned pale. "John, she is in a secure location with the queen. To bring them here would put their lives in peril."

The king breathed deeply before answering. "Thomas, I didn't ask you to bring both of them. Just bring me the witch."

The two men, friends since the king was a child, stared hard into each other's eyes.

"Be quick, Thomas, we do not have much time."

The first advisor was the first to break eye contact. "Yes, your majesty."

As his oldest friend left to summon the thaumaturge, the king turned his attention back to the valley. His commanders led their divisions forward in a measured march, conserving as much energy as possible for the fight. The Black Army hadn't bothered to do the same. They rushed at the Red Army like wolves hunting rabbits.

Though his heart ached for all his men, he reserved the worst for his sons. Memories of their childhoods came to him. Scenes of Bekitt and Erin schooling, playing, and falling in love played in his mind. The weight of knowledge that they would not survive beyond this day crushed his soul.

The Black Army's battle cry rose as they approached within striking distance. The king leaned forward, his eyes following his sons. Moments later, the two front lines collided.

Erin was the first to be struck down.

The king bowed, held his breath, shook his head, and asked

his son for forgiveness. His grief turned to anger. Inhaling, he brought one hand before his eyes and formed it into a fist. Because his men were watching him, it was no time to show weakness. He returned his gaze to the battle.

The enemy was pushing through his front lines with ease. The Black Army progressed deeper, until the king could no longer see clusters of red helmets. The sunlight flashed off the enemy's swords and shields. Triumphant shouts overpowered the screams of his dying men. Bodies littered the ground, leaving gaps among the combatants. The king counted fewer and fewer red helmets.

"Your Majesty!"

The king turned from the carnage to the voice of his first advisor.

"I have brought the thaumaturge."

A woman, cloaked from head to toe, stood before the king. She did not bow or offer a greeting. The king hurried to her. He reached out and pulled the hood back from her head. Long, wavy brown hair fell to her shoulders. While he had found her deep blue eyes, soft skin, and full lips to be arousing in the past, none of it made an impression now.

"Sorceress," he said to her, his voice high and rushed, "what can you do?"

The thaumaturge walked past the king and looked over the valley. After having scanned the battlefield, she returned to the king's side. "What would you have me do?"

The king's face turned red as his voice bellowed. "Those are the Red City's men dying down there! One of the queen's sons has died, maybe both! There must be something you can do!"

"Was it Erin?"

The king nodded.

The thaumaturge bit her lower lip and closed her eyes. A single tear slid down her right cheek. After a moment, she composed herself and addressed the king in a soft voice. "Your Majesty, the queen has commanded me not to assist you in this matter."

A coldness traveled through the king's veins. He clenched his jaws. *So my wife does have something to do with this.*

"But, Your Majesty, the Red City is my home. My father and brothers are fighting this battle for you also."

The king stared into the witch's eyes. His reply was not framed as a question. "So, you will help."

"There is always a price when sorcery is involved."

"Of course there is a price," the king replied. "There's always a price to be paid when magic is employed, but it cannot be any steeper than the one I am paying now. Use your magic, witch. Stop this madness."

The young woman nodded and stepped out to face the valley once more. She removed her cloak, dress, and any ceremonial trinkets she was wearing. The king gasped when he saw long scars traveling down the back of her arms and thighs.

"I am Bellonarii," she shouted to the sky, "I request favor!"

Clouds gathered above them, and a wind blew from the north. The king's bodyguards turned to him in wonder and distress. He ignored them and focused on his queen's thaumaturge.

The witch went to her knees and raised her head. She lifted her arms high and spoke.

"Bellona, Empress of the Sabine, Consort of Nerio, I beseech you for assistance. Our land is being taken from us. This is not war, empress. This is slaughter. Allow our families to be safe and whole."

The witch stood and crossed her arms at the wrists. Shouting to the skies, she chanted.

*"Lift our spirits*
*Let the Red City win this battle*
*And then, with the gratitude of our king,*
*Allow those of our bloodline*
*To return to their families."*

The clouds receded, the wind vanished. The king's eyes remained on the thaumaturge.

She turned, picked up her clothing, dressed, put her trinkets on, and slipped into her cloak. After sliding the hood over her head, she approached him. "It is done, Your Majesty. Give it a few moments. I take my leave."

As she turned, the king called out to her. "Where will you go?"

With her back to him, she replied. "I have betrayed my queen. I go to my family's home. I will wait."

The enormity of what the thaumaturge had done struck the king. If the battle did turn, he pledged to reward her for her assistance.

The king, his first advisor, and his bodyguards faced the battlefield. The valley was a sea of black helmets. The roar of the Black Army was almost deafening as they slashed and hacked away at his men. A few moments were an eternity to the king.

As they all beheld the battlefield, the king noticed a change. The shouts and celebrations of the Black Army were less intense. The swinging of their swords diminished. Their movements slower.

His first advisor spoke. "It's working. The witch's spell is working!"

Soon, all activity by the Black Army ceased. From what the king and his men on the hill could discern, the Black Army's soldiers were gazing at their feet.

Among the Black Army, a sea of red helmets sprouted.

The fallen were rising.

The resurrected soldiers lifted their weapons, thrust them high into the air, and then tore into their enemy.

Screams pierced the ears of the king and his men.

The sheer numbers of the Black Army insured that they would not go down easily. Their swords slashed into the bodies of the dead, but their victims did not drop. Amputated limbs sailed through the air, but the Red Army battled on, using their teeth and whatever else remained to tear their foes apart. The resurrected soldiers fought with a fury that the king knew would not be possible if they were alive. The black helmets who sought to escape were chased down—the ground bloody in their wake. In a short time, only red helmets remained upright.

The dead soldiers of the Red Army surveyed the battlefield. Satisfied their enemy had been conquered, as one, they snapped their heads toward the king.

The king and his group had not spoken since the first advisor had announced the spell was working. Now that victory was theirs, all of them had one question.

*What now?*

A group of red helmets, no more than thirty, split from the battlefield and gathered. From what the king could determine, these soldiers were whole, alive. They engaged in conversation among themselves. Their talk was animated and lasted several minutes. One of them left the group and approached the dead army. The resurrected drew themselves in tighter. One of them broke from their ranks and moved toward the living soldier. The two met and another conversation ensued. Minutes passed, and then, the living soldier placed his arms on the shoulders of his dead comrade. They both nodded and returned to their respective groups. After more conversation among themselves, all of the living soldiers walked to the dead army and formed a line in front of them. Side by side, the living soldiers walked toward the king. The army of the dead followed.

The king's head tilted as he surveyed the battlefield. A dozen or so bodies wearing red helmets remained on the ground.

*Not all of them had been resurrected.*

The living soldiers came to a halt within speaking distance of the king. They parted, allowing him visual access to the risen dead. He searched the resurrected army, seeking his sons. His eyes rested on his youngest. The king's chest tightened. His legs weakened. Groaning, he slipped toward the ground. His bodyguards rushed to support him.

Erin broke from the mob and approached.

Below the knee, a bone jutted from Erin's right leg. His right ankle was so badly broken that his foot had turned sideways. Both his arms were severed—the left below the shoulder, and the right above his elbow. Though his face was recognizable, it did not escape damage—a black hole was the only evidence of a right eye. His throat was untouched, allowing Erin to address the king. He uttered one word.

"Father."

Tears clung to the king's cheeks. He shrugged off his bodyguards and stood. He reached with fingers bent like claws to his son. "I am so sorry, Erin."

His son replied with a nod.

"Bekitt," asked the king, "what of Bekitt?"

Erin twisted his body and nodded once more, this time to the bodies wearing red helmets that remained on the battlefield. "I don't understand. Why hasn't Bekitt risen?"

Erin spoke, his voice distant, hollow. "Father, those of us slain found ourselves in a void. We were called, told to follow a light. As we moved toward it, someone called us back. It was a woman's voice. It said in part, '...allow those of our bloodline to return to their homes'."

The king's eyes narrowed, a frown dressed his lips. After a moment's thought, his eyes grew wide, his teeth clenched. Two words his son spoke echoed in his head...*our bloodline*. Though the king had his answer to his wife's loyalty to the Red City, he now knew her betrayal extended beyond that.

"Father." His son's voice brought him back to the present. "We have done what we have been tasked. We have won the battle for the Red City."

"Yes," the king replied, "you have saved us. I ask you, Erin, what happens next?"

"Our bodies have no life blood lifeblood to sustain us. We are rotting. We have only days before we are no more. We ask to fulfill the remaining task given to us. With the gratitude of our king, we wish to return home to our wives, our children, and our mothers and fathers."

The king's gaze went to the army of the dead. All were blood-drenched, a large number limbless, and their bodies crushed to pulp where they were trampled. Many of their faces were disfigured, some to the point where they were unrecognizable. The trauma to their families would be unimaginable. There would be no welcoming. Only grief. Only horror. The king imagined their wives recoiling in terror, their screams would echo through the city. He turned his head past them to the battlefield—to the bodies wearing red helmets not of their bloodline. His thoughts went to Bekitt. Then, they went to his queen. After a few moments, he spoke.

"Erin. Fulfill your last task. You have my eternal gratitude."

"And the others?"

The king reached out and clasped his son's shoulders. "Though they have made the ultimate sacrifice for our city, I cannot allow them to return to their homes and loved ones. Their tasks are complete."

A commotion rose behind Erin. The king lifted his gaze. The dead of the Red Army were falling—their helmets, swords, and shields brushing against each other as they collapsed. With a whisper, the king added, "Let them follow the light in peace."

With a single purpose, Erin brushed past his father to complete his journey home. The living followed. The king, first in line behind his son, could not conceal his grin.

# STORY NOTES (BLUE STARS)

*I*had read a collection by Mercedes Yardley called **Beautiful Sorrows**, *which contained a number of stories involving stars (dead planets). I loved the idea of how stars could play an important part of a narrative. Mercedes' wondrous stories inspired me to try my hand at it. The first story I wrote using her unique device was called "Stardust" (The Seeds of Nightmares), and I am proud to say it is often cited as a fan favorite. But, it wasn't enough, I wanted to explore the subject further. So one warm spring day, I sat down and typed the words Blue Stars at the top of my computer screen, and the story came pouring out of me.*

*"Blue Stars" tells the story of a naïve waitress who comes to the aid of a homeless man. The waitress is a character I borrowed from my then novel-in-progress called* **The Moore House***. Her name is Sandi, and she is loosely based on a member of my writers' group. Another member's name in my writers' group, Robert Perreault, was used for the school mentioned. Finally, a character I had created in an earlier short story (who was also a major player in* **The Moore House***) was a perfect fit in the tale, so the pawnshop owner also makes an appearance in "Blue Stars".*

*When I brought the finished work to my writers' group, their reaction was off the chart. I knew I had written something special. I held onto "Blue Stars" after it was done, vowing to submit it to a pro-paying anthology. It was not to be.*

*I am a huge fan of the annual gathering of horror and genre writers called Necon. At the time of this publication, I will have attended nine Necons. Each one of them has changed my life for the better. In 2016, it was announced that Necon would be publishing a charity anthology called* Now I Lay Me Down to Sleep *to benefit The Dana Farber Institute, and The Jimmy Fund. The editors, Laura Hickman and P.D. Cacek, were accepting blind submissions through Matt Bechtel, one of the principals of Necon. Since this was a charitable anthology, the writers would not be compensated.*

*I admit to hesitating to submit "Blue Stars," but not because I wanted to get paid. "Blue Stars" was dark, containing mature content. Parents of sick children would be reading this anthology, and I debated if it was appropriate to send it. In the end, I thought the decision should be made by the editors. If "Blue Stars" was accepted, it was a way for me to pay my Necon good fortune forward.*

*When Necon announced "Blue Stars" made the anthology, I beamed with pride. It's often cited as the best short I have written. Maybe it is.*

# BLUE STARS

Though I had been waitressing for only a couple of days, I had seen my fair share of characters eating breakfast at the diner. You couldn't always tell them from the way they looked, but there was no mistaking it when they opened their mouths. They were loud, often glad-handing anyone in the path to their seats. I imagined that in the reality show playing in their heads, they had the starring role. Staff, customers—we all played along—returning their greetings with a smile, an exaggerated guffaw, or a pat on the back. But when the tall man walked in, the decibel level in the diner dropped so low you would have thought a church service had commenced.

I said the tall man walked in, but *shuffled* in might be a better description. His shoes made a squeaking sound as one foot, then the other, slid across the tiled floor. With his head low, he got as far as the cash register before he paused. He lifted his chin and surveyed the diner before his gaze fixed on a booth in Roxanne's section, a far corner where there were few customers. I followed him with my eyes as he made his way there. His hair was clean but unkempt, as was his beard. He was dressed for the morning chill of an early May day, donning a full-length, well-worn London Fog coat, though it was stained and the bottom was frayed. The left pocket was torn and folded over. As soon as he sat down, the church service must have been over, because the customers went back to chitchatting and eating their eggs and bacon as loudly as before.

"Honey, that one's yours."

I turned and saw Roxanne behind me, her head nodding in the direction of the tall man. "But that's your section," I replied, not bothering to hide the frown on my face.

"You're the new girl. The new girl always has to wait on Edgar. And, he will continue to be your customer until there's another new girl." Roxanne had started at The Goffstown Diner a month before I did, and I had caught a sense of relief in her voice.

The customers' reaction and Roxanne's comments had made me apprehensive about waiting on him. As a delaying tactic, I grabbed a pot of coffee and offered to fill my customers' empty cups, and promised them more toast and additional ketchup. Then, I took a deep breath and held it before I slipped through the maze of tables over to the tall man.

His head was bent, his eyes fixed on the empty table. Standing at his booth, I placed the coffeepot down, removed a menu from my apron and placed it in front of him. It wasn't there for more than a second before he raised his head and turned it toward me. I took a step back.

The tall man's sealed lips betrayed no emotion—a sharp contrast to the rest of his face. Wrinkles creased his forehead. A ruddy nose and cheeks evidenced he spent some time outdoors. His dark brown eyes, opened wide, reflected the fluorescent lights. Vacant and cold, they drilled into mine with precision, causing me to freeze in place. When he spoke, I had to ask him to repeat himself.

"I would like a cup of blue stars," he said, his voice faint but even. The corners of his mouth dropped, his eyes softened, and his voice cracked when he added, "please?"

As his eyes bored into mine, I couldn't look away. I had no idea what a cup of blue stars was, and I was reluctant to confess that to him. However, as sad as he appeared, I caught the hopefulness in his request. How would he react if he didn't like my answer? Would he cause a scene?

"Um, let me check, I'll be right back." It was all I thought to say. I picked up the coffeepot and headed toward the kitchen.

Roxanne was at the counter window waiting for Chris, the owner and chef, to load up a plate. "Hey," I said to her, "that guy, Edgar, was asking for a cup of blue stars. What the heck are those?"

Roxanne turned to me. Looking down her nose, she grunted. "Give him a cup of hot coffee and then leave the table." She scooped up a plate from the counter and waded back into the jumble of customers.

I swung my head over to the tall man's booth. He was staring at me with that same sad but hopeful expression he had when I left him. I walked to the coffee machine, exchanged pots, and poured a mug of black coffee. As I approached his table, I hoped the mug of coffee would satisfy him. When I placed it down, his faced dropped. He gazed absently at the mug without a word.

As much as I wanted to question him, I had other customers and couldn't spare the time. I hustled over to my section and went back to work.

Before I knew it, it was ten-thirty—time for the lunch shift to relieve me. The diner was full, and because the turnover in my section was brisk, I made some decent money. Before leaving, I turned to the booth where the tall man had sat. There were a man and a woman there, drinking coffee and talking. I never saw him leave and I have no idea if he paid for his coffee.

When Roxanne and I left the diner together, I stopped her outside. The sun's glare beat down on Roxanne, so she lifted her hand to shield her eyes. "What's up, honey?"

"The tall man who walked in this morning—you called him Edgar. What's his story?"

Roxanne dropped her hand and pursed her lips. She moved to my side to hide from the sun and faced me. "Edgar was one of the French teachers at that college you go to, umm..."

"The Perreault Institute."

I am a commuting student, a freshman majoring in French at a private college here in Goffstown. My classes start in the afternoon so the hours at the diner work out perfect for me, and since I live with my parents, all my earnings go toward my education.

"Yeah, the Perreault Institute," Roxanne repeated. "Edgar Dupond is his full name. He lived in a nice house on the west side of Goffstown, near the blueberry farm. The house burned down about a year ago while he was at work. His wife survived, but his young daughter died in the blaze. You didn't read about it in the papers?"

I shook my head no.

"It was terrible. They said she hid under her parents' bed, and that she died from the fire, not the smoke. I heard from Nick, one of the firefighters, that they found her curled up in a ball.

"About six months ago his wife left him. He started showing up here and at other restaurants in town asking for a cup of blue stars. Nobody knew what to do. We called the police but they couldn't do anything if he was behaving and paying his check. And, honey, he always pays his check. He's been living across the street in an apartment on Main Street since then. The eyesore with the pawnshop out back. Over there actually." Roxanne pointed to a run-down building that housed a tavern on the main floor that the locals have dubbed *The Scum Bar*, and two stories of tenements above it.

"Anyway, he doesn't cause any trouble and Chris takes pity on him, so we leave him alone."

"You've never asked him what a cup of blue stars was?"

"Sure we have, but he never answers. He just gives you that sad, hangdog face. We've got used to him. He never has more than a cup of coffee, and he's a lousy tipper. Takes up a booth, too, during the morning rush."

I thought about what Roxanne said. "Did anyone try to help him out?"

"I don't know. Look, I gotta go. My kids are at home and I need to feed them." Without saying goodbye, Roxanne did an about-face and walked away.

Weeks went by since I first waited on the tall man, and now spring has turned to summer. School is out, and I've managed to get Chris to give me more hours. Instead of working until ten-thirty, I also work the lunch crowd now and leave at two o'clock. I continue to see the tall man, at least four times a week, and he always asks for a cup of blue stars. Today was no exception, and as usual, I disappointed him.

My shift over, I leave the diner and pause at the front door. It is a beautiful day so instead of taking a right and going straight home, I decide to detour through Main Street. I turn left and walk past The Scum Bar, the Chinese restaurant, and the laundry, toward the small park near the library. As I approach, I see the tall man sitting on one of the benches. He's staring straight ahead, and I think this is my chance to find out more about him.

"*Bonjour, Edgar! Je suis Sandi, une serveuse au restaurant. Je vous sers un café dans la matinée. Parfois.*" His head lifts and he stares at me. The expression he wears is no different than the one we see in the mornings. He does not utter a word.

"Excuse me, I thought you might be more comfortable if I spoke French, but I may be mistaken. Let me start again. Hello, Edgar! I am Sandi, a waitress at the diner who serves you coffee in the morning. Sometimes." His reaction is quick. He turns away from me.

Undeterred, I'm determined to find out more about the man. I take a seat on the bench next to him and wait. I stare into the street, mimicking his pose. We sit here for ten minutes, looking like two statues waiting for a bird to alight. Finally, he turns his head toward me, stares into my eyes for at least a minute, and then he speaks. "*M'avez-vous apporte' une tasse d'etoiles bleues?*"

Did you bring me a cup of blue stars?

I stare back. His eyebrows are raised, but his stare is unfocused. He knows the answer before I can speak it. "No," I say, switching back to English, which is more comfortable for me, "I didn't, Edgar. To tell you the truth, I don't know what a cup of blue stars is. Can you tell me?"

Edgar blinks several times. I think he's running my question through his head. He takes a small, labored breath and then faces forward again, but this time he peers down at his lap. His silence makes me nervous. Maybe I erred in asking him. As I stand to leave, Edgar speaks.

"I used to read her a story every night before she went to sleep. It was about a young girl whose father had a cup of blue stars that he had stored away for her. Whenever the young girl in the story was in trouble at school, had a falling out with a friend or was in pain, her father would reach into his cup of blue stars and give her one. The stars were magical, and they would always have the power to fix the young girl's problems. The night before my Mercedes died, she asked me if I could get her her very own cup of blue stars. She told me, with that cup, I would always be there to help her out." Edgar turns to me with that sad but hopeful face he wore in the mornings. "I need to find a cup of blue stars. It's the only way to get her back, the only way we can be together again."

Of all the explanations Edgar could have given me, I do not expect this one. I close my eyes and choke back a sob. Speechless, all I can do is reach my hand to his and grasp it. Edgar recoils at my touch. He stands with his arms by his side and shouts. "You think I'm crazy! My wife thought so, too! Maybe I am. But the hell with all of you! I know there are blue stars out there, and I'll find them!"

The outburst over, his shoulders sag and his chin dips. Lowering his voice, he adds, "I've got to see if they work."

My eyes grow moist as Edgar shuffles away from the bench.

Thoughts of Edgar and his suffering leave a hole in my soul. Emotionally unstable, he deserves assistance rather than pity. An image of his daughter dying in the fire pops into my head. It's too graphic for me to handle and I attempt to shake it out.

I leave the park and wander down Main Street, retracing my route from the diner. I make it a point to study my surroundings to keep my mind off Edgar's plight. I see a house that needs painting. The wear and rot on the clapboards conspire to convince the onlooker that the plaque on the front of the house is accurate—*Built in 1818.* Trash along the road embraces the curbing, resisting any breeze that might hustle it away. Weeds flourish, packed in tightly among sand and discarded cigarette butts. Weathered decks, held in place with sagging four-by-fours jut from the sides of turn-of-the-century apartment buildings. I know this town has a lot going for it, but at the moment, I am blind to its treasures. When I pass The Scum Bar, I decide to take a left onto a side street that follows the river. After the turn, I walk a few steps and I'm surprised to see a canopy overhanging the sidewalk. In faded black letters, the canopy advertises *Goffstown Pawn Shop.*

Roxanne mentioned the pawnshop this morning, but it hadn't registered with me. I walk toward the shop—one more diversion to put Edgar and his troubles out of my mind. When I find myself in front of it, I lean in close to the window to peek inside. The glass is tinted and all I see is my own reflection. Stepping back from the window, I look to the entrance. There are double glass doors with security cameras placed above each one. For a brief moment, I consider how I look. Turning back to the window, I assure myself that my makeup is fine despite my earlier tears, and that I don't look too frumpy in my waitress whites. After shrugging my shoulders at my reflection, I turn and enter the pawnshop.

It's nothing like I imagine it would be.

I expect a dirty, cluttered area with wobbly tables stacked high with old chainsaws, cheap stereo equipment, and well-worn household appliances. The opposite greets me. The only objects for sale in the shop are neatly stacked on wooden shelves aligned against the walls, and all those objects look more like pieces of art rather than grease-laden junk. The center of the shop is clean and vacant of shelves. It would be the perfect place for a square dance. Gazing to the left, I see a long counter that runs alongside the wall. The counter is empty, except for a man leaning on it.

"Hello, young lady! What can I do for you on this bright, sunny day?"

He is a thin man, I guess middle-aged. Nondescript with short hair. It sounds as though he has a New England accent, but for some reason it doesn't ring true with me. I chalk it up to him trying hard to make a sale.

"I'm okay, thank you for asking," I reply. My answer brought me back to Edgar and his quest. Lowering my head, I stare at my shoes for a moment before following up. "I'm only browsing, really." I return my gaze to him. "I've never been in here before."

He cocks his head and eyes me up and down. After sizing me up, he must have come to some rapid conclusion about me. "You must forgive me, Miss, but I'm fairly sure you could not afford the merchandise I carry here. But, it seems to me that you are searching for something. Maybe I could point you in the right direction." He speaks that last sentence as a fact, not a question. I warm to his confidence.

"It's silly really. I am a waitress at The Goffstown Diner and I have this customer..." I tell him Edgar's story, filling him in on everything, right up to my entering his shop. I did wipe away some stray tears by the end, but I feel good that I didn't wind up bawling like a baby.

The pawnshop owner takes his elbows off the counter and stands straight. His head is slightly tilted to the left, but he has a gleam in his eyes and a smile on his lips. "That's quite the story, Miss. I take it you want to help Edgar in his quest." Once again, it sounds like a statement, not a question.

My spirits lift. I do want to help Edgar, and the pawnshop owner understands that. He is not dismissive of my intentions. Maybe he wants to help Edgar, too?

"Yes," I answer. "But I don't know how."

"Wait there a minute."

The man ducks under the counter. I can hear him moving items around and muttering to himself. "I know I put it somewhere here," he says in a low voice, sounding annoyed. "Gosh darn it, where are you?" After I hear objects falling to the floor, he speaks up. "Yeah! Found you!" He stands up with a coffee can in his hands.

He once again leans forward with his elbows on the counter and thrusts his find toward me. Holding the can with one hand, he removes the plastic lid. He nods and tilts it so I can see inside.

I gasp.

The can is half-full of blue stars.

They are dime-sized, and when the man jiggles the coffee can, the lights above us reflect off their points. They gleam a brilliant blue. Lifting my chin, I stare at him with wide eyes. "How...?"

He finishes my sentence for me. "How did I get these? Last month I received an estate collection from a dealer in Texas. For some reason, two American flags made of copper were included. I had no use for the flags, but I knew the copper could be sold at a good price for scrap. However, the stars on the flag were made from stainless steel. I'm guessing they were not custom-made, that the artist bought them from a catalog or a supply house. I had some time so I stripped them off. Cut my fingers more than a few times getting them out. Lucky for you, I had an empty coffee can nearby to store them in; otherwise, I might have thrown them out."

"What are the chances you would have these?"

The pawnshop owner doesn't answer, instead, he grins.

"How much do you want for these?"

"Five dollars."

"You got a sale!"

It's very busy in the diner this morning, but despite the rush, I glance at the door every chance I get to see if Edgar is here. I'm so distracted that I don't hear some of my customers ordering and I have to ask them to repeat themselves. Roxanne must have noticed that I was preoccupied as she took me aside earlier to ask me if everything was okay. When I told her I was feeling great, she gave me an uplifted eyebrow and went back to work.

As I'm taking an order from regulars John and Don Sullivan, a couple who sport matching wedding rings, I hear the chit-chat in the diner quiet down. Turning toward the door, I see Edgar has arrived. He shuffles in and heads to a booth at the far side of the restaurant. My pulse races, and my hands holding the pencil and order pad tremble. Somehow, I managed to get John and Don's order down and tell them I'll be back in a minute with coffee. Instead of heading to the coffee maker, I walk over to Edgar's booth. He sits there rigid, both hands atop the table and facing the opposite side of the booth, possibly staring at something no one else can see.

"Good morning, Edgar, what can I get you?" My speech is rushed, my voice higher than normal. Edgar doesn't notice. Our conversation yesterday must not have made an impression on him either, as he repeats his request in his same lifeless monotone.

He doesn't bother to look up from the tabletop when he asks, "A cup of blue stars, please."

I linger a few heartbeats before I answer. "Yes, sir. A cup of blue stars."

Edgar lifts and cocks his head to me. He squints and studies my facial expression. My answer is not what he was expecting—he must be deciding how to react. After a few moments, the corners of his mouth sag, but I can see his gaze is softening. He's confused, but curious. I return his soft gaze, but the corners on my mouth lift. I leave to get his order.

At the counter, I grab an empty mug, bend my knees and search the shelf below for the coffee can the pawnshop owner sold me. I placed it there when I started my shift, hiding it behind a bale of napkins. The napkins moved aside, I pull the can toward me. The lid comes off easily and I pour the contents into the coffee mug. The blue stars make a tinkling sound as they fall and settle. I place the can back on the shelf and slide the napkins in front of it. Straightening up, I hold the coffee mug high so no one can see its contents, and I make my way back to Edgar.

Arriving at his booth, I see that he is still turned toward me. My hand trembles, and it's not because of the weight of the mug. I hesitate to put it on the table. Doubt races through my mind. Will he be upset? Will he think that I'm ridiculing his obsession? What if his reaction is so negative he causes a scene? Turning back is out of the question though—Edgar's gaze is fixed on me. He must see the mixture of anticipation and doubt on my face. Adjusting his position on the bench, he shifts his weight to his left bum, then his right. He continues the pattern three more times, and then sits up straight.

Frozen to the spot, I take a deep breath. I place the mug on the table, close enough where he can see the contents without having to handle it. Stepping back, I wait for his reaction.

Edgar stares at the mug for what feels like an eternity. Finally, he looks up at me for a moment, and then back down into the mug. He repeats the act without comment. I notice his arms inching their way onto the table.

Cradling the mug with his left hand, he uses his right to reach into the mug. Edgar plucks out one of the blue stars.

"Careful," I tell him, "those are sharp."

The surface of the blue star is smooth. It offers no resistance as Edgar slides it between his fingertips. His mouth is closed, but there is a smile forming on his lips. When he turns to me, the smile is complete. "Thank you," he says.

Relief washes over me as I drop my shoulders and exhale loudly. "Edgar, I'm not sure these will do what you think they will do. Maybe I'm making things worse for you, but at least your search will be over, and you'll know."

Tears flow from Edgar's eyes. They fall onto the tabletop. I watch as they meld and grow.

He turns back to the mug and speaks in a soft voice. "Thank you for allowing me to be with my Mercedes once more."

I start to reply, but he moves so fast I can't get out the words.

Edgar drops the star back into the mug. His mouth opens wide and his head tilts back. Lifting the mug in his right hand, he brings it to his lips, and pours the blue stars down his throat.

*Oh my God, what is he doing?*

My chest tightens and my brain goes numb. I'm deaf to the clatter in the diner, except for the gagging noise Edgar makes while swallowing. As cold and immobile as an ice sculpture, I stand there, unable to react. My thought process is as frozen as my body—my head empty except for a still picture of Edgar holding the mug high to his lips.

Edgar snorts, lowers the mug a few inches, and gags. A geyser of blue and red spews onto the tabletop, and my apron.

Lowering my head to the mess, I feel the world rush back at me. I shake my head, whisper, "no and then take a step toward him. Grabbing his arm, I pull the mug toward me. There are a few blue stars, mixed with blood, stuck to the bottom. Choking sounds turn my attention back to him.

Edgar's neck is a bulging column of flesh. Bumps, the size of goose pimples, appear all over. Dropping the mug, his hands fly to his throat. He wraps his hands around it, one over the other, and then he squeezes.

The points break through.

Blood seeps from the wounds.

His fingers streak red.

Somebody is screaming for help. I realize it's me. I back away from Edgar, my eyes glazing over and my head still shaking. Chairs scrape the floor and I hear dishes crashing. A pair of hands clamp onto my shoulders, moving me aside. A voice to my right exclaims, "Dear God." Edgar falls sideways out of the booth and onto the floor. His face is dark blue and his legs are thrashing. His hands continue to squeeze at his throat, until, they too, rest against the floor. His heels drum against the tiles for a few more seconds, then they still.

"Call nine-one-one!" Someone shouts.

"I don't know what to do," a man to my left confesses.

"Look at his throat. What is that?" It's Roxanne, from somewhere behind me.

I look down at Edgar's face. His eyes are wide, dull, and staring at the ceiling. A stream of blood trickles from his mouth, draining blue stars onto his beard. Their exposed surfaces catch the fluorescent light and the stars' gleam.

Customers jostle against my back. I lean into them, forcing myself backward—away from the blue stars, and the blood pooling around the body.

Away from Edgar.

Turning, I push myself through the small mob. Most of the customers in the diner are standing in my path. I bounce off them as they move toward the booth. When I break free of the crowd, I see not everyone has gone to their feet. The older customers, the ones who struggle to walk, have remained at their tables. They stare at my apron. Their faces turn to me—some with their mouths open and their faces tight, others expectant that I will fill them in on what's happening. I look away from them and hurry to the entrance of the diner.

Outside, I lean back against the wall, close my eyes and breathe deep. My reprieve is short-lived; I can hear the sirens in the distance racing to get here. As bad as I feel for Edgar, my thoughts turn to my own situation. There will be questions. I wonder if I could wind up in jail.

When the ambulance pulls up to the diner, its piercing siren forces my eyes open. As the EMTs rush inside, I see a thin middle-aged man off to the side.

The pawnshop owner is leaning against a car with a grin, his eyes trained on me.

"How'd those blue stars work out for you?" he asks me.

# STORY NOTES (EYES)

*I*started "Eyes" in 2007, and it took me ten years to finish it.
I had written a few stories by then, and I wanted to experiment with a narrative that was new to me. A first-person narration came to mind, and I decided all the sentences would be in dialogue. Things went along well—the story came easily and I was pleased with the results. But, I had a major problem.

My main character was talking in the present tense. Not only that, but I had other characters speaking back to him, some of whose discussions referenced events in the past. To make matters worse, those events in the past had characters speaking in the present. Structurally it worked, but I was so confused as to where to put quotation marks.

I asked some friends for help, but no one could say for sure how to do it. When attending the MoCon convention in 2007, I asked Tom Piccirilli, Gerard Houarner, Linda Addison, and Kelli Owen for advice. Coming back from the convention, I tried to use their words of wisdom, but it still didn't feel right.

I put the story away, taking it out occasionally over the years to fiddle with it. The breakthrough came in 2017, long after I had joined a writers' group. Robert Perreault, a French-language professor at a local college who was a member of my writers' group, asked to look at it. He explained what should be done, took it home, edited it, and handed it back to me. I was stunned at the results. Bob made it all work! It was now ready to submit.

The first time I submitted it, the publisher rejected it, explaining while it was a good and interesting story, it didn't fit in with his anthology. I understood, but was crushed.

*A short time later, Phil Perron with Great Old Ones publishing contacted me. He invited me to submit to his newest anthology called* Invocations. *It was amazing as "Eyes" met all the criteria he was looking for in his call. I sent it to him, and his editor, Gregory Norris, accepted the story. After ten years, "Eyes" found a home.*

# EYES

Hey there, young lady, how you doing? You waiting for someone? No? Mind if I sit down? What are you drinking? Let me order one for you. Have you got a few minutes? Could I tell you a story? Great! It's about this guy who lives in the apartment next to me. His name is Steve.

Steve can't see very well. I don't mean he's blind, but he's always bumping into things or asking the neighbors to read his mail for him. Sometimes, he has trouble getting his key into his door lock. Steve can be a pain in the butt, but all of us in the apartment complex put up with him because he's a nice guy. It's not like he leaves his garbage in the hall or blasts his TV. No, Steve's pretty well behaved.

Something else you should know about Steve—he's always broke. The guy doesn't have a pot to piss in, really. He can't find a job because his eyesight is so bad. Don't ask me how he gets by with what the State of New Hampshire gives him every month for disability, but somehow the guy pays his rent. I guess living in subsidized housing helps. And since Steve hasn't got a job, he doesn't have any insurance either, so that means no eye exams or glasses.

So anyway, I was coming home from work this afternoon and I saw him walking down the hallway, and guess what? He wasn't bumping into anything! He had mail in his hand and it looked like he was reading it. I must have laughed because he turned around to look at me, and wow, he had glasses on!

"Hey, four eyes!" I called to him. "Where'd you get the glasses?" He lifted his head, gave me this goofy smile and waved me into his apartment. "Hell, have I got a story for you, man," he said back at me.

Steve let me in, led me over to his kitchen and we sat down. That's when I got a good look at his new specs.

It wasn't his own eyes staring back at me.

Somebody had painted these two big eyeballs right on the lenses. Whoever painted them did a pretty good job though. They'd almost look like real peepers if they weren't so big.

"Can you see out of those things?" I asked him. He laughed like crazy. And get this, no matter which way he moved his head, those painted-on eyeballs kept staring at me.

His laughter died down and then he got real serious. He leaned over and said, "You're not going to believe this, Derek!"

That's my name by the way. Derek. It's nice to meet you. I guess I should have told you that after I sat down.

Well, to continue with my story, Steve said to me, "Two days ago there's this knock on my door. I opened it, and even though I can't see good more n' a foot in front of me, there, as clear as freaking day, I saw this beautiful broad standing in the hallway! It was funny because everything else around her was foggy as usual, but hell, not her. And man, was she gorgeous! It's like she walked right out of the pages of *Playboy*, except she had her clothes on. Too bad," he added, "she had great knockers."

Steve looked past me, dropped his shoulders and sighed. He must have been visualizing that woman's big chest.

"Where was I?" he said, turning to me again. "Oh yeah, she just stood there in the hallway with this big freaking grin on her face. She was wearing a short black dress, F-me shoes, and she was holding this steel briefcase."

Steve paused for a second. I guess he wanted me to get the picture. The whole time I watched him, those painted-on eyeballs kept staring back at me.

"Well, this broad didn't say a thing," Steve started back up. "She just reached out, pushed the door open more, stepped around me and walked into my apartment. Made a beeline right to my kitchen, sat down in one of the chairs and put her briefcase on the table. Then, with that big grin on her face, she waved a finger at me to come sit next to her.

"Man, I didn't know what to do at first," Steve confided to me. "But hey, how many times does a good-looking broad come knocking on my door? I said to myself, what the hell, I'm game. I would have barked like a dog if she had wanted me to. So I sat down. Man, I couldn't believe I could see her so good. She was so beautiful that I got a little uncomfortable."

Steve poked me in the ribs and made his eyebrows go up and down.

I have to admit, Miss...oh, I never asked you your name! Sandi! Great name, I love the beach. Anyway, I was a little annoyed because I don't like to be touched by a guy, but I didn't say anything. I wanted him to get back to his story. Steve must have seen that I wasn't too happy about being touched because he started talking again.

"I was going to ask her what she was doing in my apartment, how come I could see her so good, and what was in the briefcase. But, before I could get the first word out, she shook her head *no*."

Steve leaned toward me and said real serious, "Derek, this broad wanted to get right down to business."

I nodded my head at him like I knew what he was talking about. He took a deep breath before he started up again.

"The broad says to me, 'Steve, I know you have bad eyesight.' And oh my God, Derek, her voice was as smooth as topshelf scotch, I swear!"

Steve's own voice got a little softer when he told me that, but then it went back to normal.

"'Steve,' she says, 'I can fix that for you. I'm a witch. Not an evil witch, but a nice witch. I have a pair of glasses, some herbs, and a spell ritual I can perform that will let you see perfectly. Your eyesight will be so good, you'll be able to clearly see a batter hit a baseball out of the park on TV! You'll see so well you could read all the books you want without ever squinting!'"

Steve sat back grinning as he recalled the conversation. "Derek, I sure as hell know I ain't smart enough to be reading all them books. But you know, I really do miss watching the Red Sox on the tube. So, I got to thinking, what would glasses like these run me? Shoot, I knew even if those glasses were for real there was no way I could spring for 'em."

He chuckled when he told me that last part.

Resigned to the fact that he would never be able to pay for something like this, Steve told me he stood up and said to her straight away, "I'm sorry Miss, but I don't have that kind of money to... "

The witch interrupted him. "It doesn't cost any money at all, Steve. I'm a good witch! I do this out of the kindness of my heart. There is one thing you should know though. Once you agree to take possession of the glasses, if at any time you take them off you will be completely blind, but it's only temporary. That means when you take them off to shower or go to bed at night, you will see nothing, only darkness. But, put them back on after you dry off or when you wake up, you will have 20/20 vision again."

Steve said he thought about it, but not for long.

"Just think about it, Derek. I'd be able to read a newspaper or a magazine without a magnifying glass. No more worrying about being ripped off from cashiers because I can't see the numbers on the money they give me back. Most of all, I'd be able to see women again. And, if half of them are as good-looking as that witch was, shoot, the decision was a no brainer."

"Okay," Steve said to her, "as long as I don't have to pay for 'em with money or promise you my soul or nothing."

"This won't cost you any money," she replied. "And, you can keep your soul. I'm a witch, not the devil. Now sit up straight in the chair and lean your head back as far as it will go. I'm going to put some magic drops in your eyes, and don't worry, it won't hurt a bit."

After he told me this, Steve squirmed in his chair. He looked down into his lap, and I tell you, Sandi, I was relieved that those freaky-looking eyeballs were finally pointed somewhere else. But, I had the feeling they struggled like hell to look back up at me.

"So I leaned my head back, Derek," Steve said with his voice trailing off, "but not all the way, I wanted to see what this witch was up to."

Steve was lost in his thoughts for a few seconds. I wondered if he even remembered he was telling me the story.

"She stood and turned her back to me. I heard two snaps.

I guess she opened the steel case. Out of the corner of my eye, I saw her arm go into the case, and it returned with a small jar that she put on the table. I could barely see it, Derek, but it looked to be filled with some clear, watery stuff. After that, she went back into the briefcase and pulled out a pair of glasses and put them next to the jar.

"She lifted the jar and took the cap off. Then, she dipped this thing into it that must have been an eyedropper. After the witch sucked up what she needed, she got behind me with the jar in one hand and the eyedropper thingy in the other. The witch looked down at me and said, 'You ready?'"

Steve imitated the nod he gave her, and then he said she forced his head back as far as it would go.

"I was scared, Derek. I wondered what the heck I was doing. I had a whole lot of questions to ask this broad. Like, what the hell was she going to do to me? How did she find me in the first place? And how did she know my name? Shoot, I didn't even know *her* name! she really a witch? She must have seen I was scared because she smiled at me. Even looking at her upside down, she was still so freaking beautiful. Then she said to me, 'Don't worry, Steve, nothing bad is going to happen to you. I will explain everything when I'm done.'"

"She went to work on me," Steve said, "and she started out by saying some kind of weird poem out loud."

*Accept this offering, oh lord*
*Though born from sacrifice*
*It is willfully given*
*An eye for an eye*
*For this man's fortune*
*An eye for an eye*
*For this woman's absolution*

"When she was finished, she squeezed the eyedropper thingy and that clear stuff dripped into both my eyes. It was kind of warm and grainy, like it had little bits of sand in it. After it hit my eyeballs, everything went black. Derek, I couldn't see crap anymore, nothing at all out of both eyes. I wanted to scream! Then my face got all tingly. I had opened my mouth to say something, but the witch shushed me. She said everything would be fine in a few minutes. I thought her voice had been awfully close, like she had leaned right down into my face. Something hot brushed against my forehead, I wondered if it was her breath. Was she going to kiss me? Man, I had hoped so. But, something else happened. Even with my face all tingly, I had felt a tickle. Something wet slid down my cheek. It might have been some of that clear watery stuff she put into my eyes. Whatever it was, it had worked its way down to my mouth and went into my lips. It tasted sweet.

"She must have put the eyedropper thingy down somewhere because one of her hands grabbed my chin. She held it so I wouldn't move my head. She put something on my left eye. It wasn't heavy, but hell, it moved around a lot. It was soft and wet at the same time. I was thinking maybe she was kissing my eye. Then I heard this noise above my face. I could have sworn it sounded like what you hear when you're sucking down a Coke with a straw and you get to the bottom of the cup. Right after I heard that noise, there was a tugging, then a popping sound. And you know what? The weight on my eye was gone! Right after that, I heard what sounded like spitting, and then a small splash.

"She did the same thing to my right eye.

"After I heard a second splash, she breathed into my ear and said, 'Almost done, Steve.'"

"She must have had a sponge with her because she wiped around my eyes. I thought she must have been mopping up some of that clear watery stuff, though I could have sworn I'd heard some more weird noises, almost like lips smacking. She whispered into my ear, and Derek, it was as soft a cat's purr. She said, 'I am going to put the glasses on you now.'"

Well, I'll tell you, Sandy, I was pretty creeped out by Steve's story by then. I thought about high-tailing it out of there. He must have seen that I had a pretty disgusted look on my face because he stood straight up and put his arm on my shoulder. Steve held me down and looked me straight in the eyes with those new glasses. Those big painted-on eyeballs were only inches from mine. He said, "Derek, it was freaking unbelievable.

I could see! Everything around me was as clear as a bell. Well... except for the witch.

"She was all hazy, like the way I saw everything before she put those glasses on me. But I could see everything else in the apartment, and man, it was clear as day. I was so excited, Derek, that I walked around looking at stuff. I saw the hands on my clock. I could see the numbers on the remote control. Shoot, I even read the back of my Cheerios box! I saw everything real good—except for her.

"Then I heard her putting all her stuff back into the steel case. I saw the jar in her hands, and looking at it, I got a little dizzy. Two small round things were floating around in there. I couldn't look at it, Derek. I didn't want to know what those things were."

Steve paused, and then sat back.

"She finished putting her stuff into the case, then closed it and walked to the door. 'Hey, wait a sec,' I said to her, 'you told me you would tell me why you helped me!'"

Now if you've been following my story here, Sandi, you sure as heck know as well as I do what Steve saw floating around in that jar. I don't blame him. I would have felt a little sick, too. But, I put that out of my mind. I wanted to find out more about this witch. It was my turn to lean forward, and I looked Steve right in those funky eyeballs and asked him what she told him.

"Get this, Derek" he tells me. "She stopped, turned to me and said, 'Well, Steve, my name is Mary Johnson. As to why I'm doing this for you, let's just say that this is my penance. A long time ago, I was part of something I never should have become involved in. I pledged my soul to another for extraordinary gifts. I had made a mistake. But, by using those gifts to help others, I can postpone my fate of eternal suffering. Hopefully, it will buy me more time to figure a way out of my situation.'"

"The witch walked to the door, and before she left, she told me that she's going to be here for a while doing what she does. You know, her penance. She said she wanted to help other people, and if I knew anyone in the building who could use her talents, I should let them know she's here. Hey, by the way, Derek, how's your eyesight? Do you need glasses?'"

Well, Sandi, when Steve finished his story and asked me those questions, two things came to mind. The first was that Steve was absolutely nuts. He must have gone crazy being almost blind and living alone in that apartment for all those years. But, there was no way I was going to ask him to take those glasses off to find out. My second thought was that maybe it was all some kind of a joke, that he put this story together just to screw with me. Since I wasn't sure which of the two it was, I decided to cover both of my bases by laughing and telling him my eyesight was fine. Without saying another word to Steve, I got up from the chair and left his apartment.

As I was leaving, I was still thinking of the jar in that woman's briefcase and I guess I was distracted. When I walked out of the door to Steve's apartment, I bumped right into Joyce. Joyce lives across the hall from Steve.

I grabbed her to keep her from falling and started to excuse myself, but I stopped in mid-sentence because I remembered that Joyce was deaf. Sandi, that woman wouldn't have heard a cannon firing if she was standing right next to it. I focused on her eyes so I could mouth the words, "I'm sorry." But when I saw her face, I gasped and threw myself back against Steve's door. It was unreal! Joyce had these two huge plastic ears attached to the sides of her head.

"J-J-J-Joyce." I stammered. "Your ears!"

"Oh yes, Derek, isn't it wonderful?" she said. "I can hear perfectly now! I met this woman, a witch, who cured my deafness! In fact, she asked about you. You see, last night there was this knock on my door and...hey, look! What do you know? There she is, at the end of the hallway!"

I pulled myself away from Steve's door and turned to look. Steve was right, man, she was beautiful!

Joyce gave me this knowing smile, mumbled something about not being able to hear the woman anymore, and turned around and let herself into her apartment.

The witch walked toward me, the steel briefcase swung in one of her hands. She stopped just a few feet from me and said, "Hello, Derek."

"Hey look," I told her, "I'm, ugh, fine. I don't need anything."

"Are you sure about that, Derek? Then why is it you live alone? Why is it you never go to the bars? Maybe bring a woman back to your apartment at the end of the night? How come you never met that someone special? Got married, had kids? You see, Derek, I know why."

I swallowed hard, and waited for her to continue.

"You were in the military, Afghanistan, wasn't it? You were in a jeep that ran over an IED. You were severely injured and they didn't know if you were going to make it, but you fought for your life. You didn't die. But a part of you did, didn't it, Derek?" She must have caught me looking at my crotch because then she said, "I thought so."

I turned and walked away from her. I'm not sure if it was because I was scared of her or because I was embarrassed she knew so much about me. When I came to my door she called out, "Derek, let's talk. There's no harm in just talking, is there?"

I thought about it for a minute, recalling Steve's story and my run-in with Joyce. What the heck? Talking with her wouldn't hurt. I invited her into my apartment. She spent the whole afternoon with me, and told me everything about herself. And, wow, she had quite the story to tell.

Hey, Sandi, I see you've finished your drink! How about letting me order you one more? After that, how would you like to come back to my place? I don't mind telling you, it's been a while since I had someone over.

# STORY NOTES (INCIDENT ON N.H. ROUTE 666)

M.J. (Mark) Preston, a writer, publisher, and good friend, invited me to contribute to his new anthology called **Dark Passages** 2. It was themed, and he called for stories involving traveling on the road. Normally, I don't accept invitations to themed anthologies—it's difficult for me to write a story with plot limitations—but as I mentioned, M.J. is my friend, and I wanted to be part of his anthology.

Thinking about it for a few days, an image of a truck driver coming up on an exorcism in the middle of the road came to me. I liked the idea and put it to paper. It was an unusually quick story—I believe it took me a month. Happy with it, I submitted.

Mark contacted me right away. He enjoyed the tale, but informed me I had a few of the technical details wrong on driving a truck. He filled me in on the jargon and mechanics on how to get a semi barreling down a highway to brake without jackknifing. And he pointed out that a truck driver would use much stronger curse words than the ones I used.

When the anthology was published, the format delighted me. Mark printed the anthology in the style of a magazine with oversized paper, a stunning gloss cover, and the stories laid out in columns. In addition, he had ads for the writers' other publications scattered among the pages.

I did make one change to the story you hold in your hands. Originally, it was titled, "Incident on N.H. Route 66". I regretted not adding the extra six, so I added it here. My thinking at the time was that no state would have a route numbered 666. As I mentioned, it bugged the hell out of me, and this is my chance to make things right.

# INCIDENT ON N.H. ROUTE 666

**❏❏**...yes, honey, I'm almost there. I'm in New Hampshire now, on this godforsaken back road. It's not even on my GPS. Radio is out, too. Not sure why since I can still talk with you on the phone."

"Not on your GPS? How'd you find it?"

"Dispatch gave me the directions. She said the pickup is in the middle of nowhere. She was right about that—I haven't seen another car or truck for half an hour."

"You empty?"

"No. She had me pick up a load of computers in Maryland first, then she sent me way the hell up here. Believe me, I'm going to have some words with her about this."

"How much longer before you get there?"

"About forty-five minutes, I think."

"Make sure you eat dinner, dear. You know how irritated you get when you don't."

"After I'm loaded, I'll take a break, then heat up something before I head home."

"What are you picking up?"

"Tractor equipment at a John Deere factory. She said it will fill the truck. I'm offloading both stops at the terminal back home."

"Oh, good. I'm taking Sue and Bobbie out to Burger King for dinner, so if you call this evening, we might not be home yet."

"If not, I'll leave a message and... HOLY SHIT!"

The truck driver froze in his seat, focused on the road ahead. Reflexes, honed from more than thirty years on the road, engaged, sending a jolt of electricity up his spine.

His grip on the phone loosened and his hand shot forward. Before the device hit the floor, he grabbed the steering wheel with both hands. Cramps shot through his fingers, turning his knuckles white. His right foot swung from the accelerator and jammed on the brake. With his back stiffening, he rode up the seat as he put everything he had on the pedal. The smoke from the air brakes drove spikes into his nostrils. The cab shuddered. He glanced at the side mirror—the trailer was sliding to the left. It was going to jackknife. The driver let up on the brakes, gave the engine a shot of fuel, and doubled down on the clutch. The gears clunked angrily and the engine howled in protest.

*Fuck, fuck, fuck, I'm not going to stop in time!*

His eyes tightened and he held his breath. The gears caught, and he slammed his foot back onto the brake pedal. Adrenalin surged through his veins—he couldn't stop shaking.

The tractor-trailer was barreling toward three people standing in the middle of his lane.

Steering left or right into the woods might have saved them, but at this speed, and the heavy oaks and pines that lined the narrow road, there was no doubt they would be picking *him* up in pieces. Doubling down on the clutch and braking might have been too little too late, but he would live to drive again. He had made his decision, and he would know in seconds if it was the right one.

As the truck rushed toward the three people, doubt hammered away at him. Why didn't they run? He closed his eyes, unwilling to witness the inevitable, and waited for the impact. When the truck screeched to a halt, forward momentum tested the strength of his seat belt. His head whipped forward and then ricocheted back, slamming against the headrest. He groaned, and then lay against the seat to wait out the shakes and the pain. Fingers to his neck, he massaged the muscles. After a moment, thoughts of the people in the road came back to him. Had he hit them? He couldn't recall an impact. Opening his eyes, he peered at the front end of his cab. Three people, standing upright, peered back at him over the hood.

Three faces. A young man and an older man stood with their mouths agape and their eyes wide open. The third, a young woman, stared at him with a neutral expression. While waiting for his heartbeat to slow and his legs to stop shaking, the trucker studied them. Something was odd. It took him a moment, but he figured out what it was. Judging from his black suit coat and the white square on the collar around his neck, the older man was a priest. Instead of imparting a sense of security that a man of the cloth was present, it induced disquiet in the trucker. When the young girl raised her hand, pointed at the priest and then screamed, the trucker jumped in his seat.

The pain in his neck forgotten, the trucker unhitched his seat belt, leaned over, and reached under the seat. His fingers wrapped around the handle of the Colt. With a practiced move, he unsnapped the Velcro hold and slid the gun out from the harness.

He tucked the pistol into the back of his pants, then reached over and turned his flashers on. He left the cab door open when he stepped onto the road. More out of habit than concern, he swung his gaze to the trailer. The stink from the airbrakes lingered, but the smoke was gone. Otherwise, it looked to be fine. The first order of business was to get these people out of the way so he could move his trailer to the side, or better yet, get the hell out of here. With the way this young woman continued to scream, he didn't have much hope of leaving the scene soon.

The trucker turned back to the cab and searched the floor, fumbling for his phone. Wedged beneath the accelerator, it didn't appear to be broken; however, he had no reception. While it did occur to him that it was strange since he had no problem talking with his wife seconds ago, the young woman's shouts interrupted his train of thought. He threw the phone onto the seat and walked to the front of the cab.

The younger man now held the woman. He was behind her, his hands wrapped around her stomach. Her arms were flailing.

"Mister, help me, please! They've raped me!"

The younger man shook his head. "What? No! No! That didn't happen! You can't pay attention to her, she's sick in the head. We're trying to help her!"

The trucker reached behind him and placed his hand over the handle of the gun. Without drawing it, he asked the priest what was going on.

The priest took a deep breath as he peered into the driver's eyes. He lifted his left hand and the trucker saw it held a Bible. "I am Father Mark, from Saint Frances Parish, over in Stonewall. You, sir, have stumbled onto an exorcism. I understand how difficult it will be for you to believe us, but it is the truth. You have put yourself and the young lady in harm's way. I would ask that you leave, and let us continue on with our task."

The trucker stared at the priest. *What the hell have I stumbled into?*

The young woman's response was swift. "What? That's a load of horseshit! The bastard holding me is my brother, and that lying sack of shit isn't really a priest. He paid my brother to rape me while he carried out his fucking perverted role-playing. They took turns on me! Please, mister, you gotta help me!"

The man holding her removed one arm from her waist and slapped her along the side of her head. "Karen, stop it! None of that is true!"

The trucker pulled the gun from his back and aimed it at the man. "You hit her one more time, I'll make sure you never do it again."

The young man pleaded. "Look, I'm telling you the truth! My name is Scott Hudson, and this here's my wife, Karen. She's possessed by the devil! The father here is trying to drive the evil out of her."

"It's true."

The trucker turned to the priest.

"Scott and Karen are members of our church. Karen began acting strangely weeks ago. She talked in tongues, fornicated with animals, and desecrated the church with pornographic images. While those symptoms could be associated with mental illness, the physical manifestations could not be. I have witnessed her hanging from walls without mechanical support, and I've seen her suspended naked in the air without attachments. I've also seen her perform remarkable feats of strength such as pushing a tractor out of her way as if it were made of cardboard, and I watched her kill a bull with one punch. There is no doubt she is possessed by a demon."

"That's all bullshit, mister! That stuff never happened!" The young woman's voice sounded incredulous. "Seriously, you can't believe this shit!"

The truck driver stared at her. After thinking for a few seconds, he asked Father Mark, "Why are you out here in the middle of the road?"

"I petitioned the church for an exorcism last week, but those wheels turn slowly. Her behavior has become worse since then. Though the local authorities have no evidence yet to implicate Karen, neighbors' livestock are being horribly butchered, homes have been vandalized with occult markings, and worse, children have reported being molested by a woman who is facially disfigured. Scott has found items in his house that tie directly to each of these crimes. He told me this morning about getting rid of the evidence, and begged me to do something now, before someone's life is lost. Though I have never performed an exorcism, I had attended a few. In light of the escalation of the demon's actions, I felt the need to attempt the ceremony on my own. We tied Karen up earlier..."

The young woman shouted an interruption. "Yeah, they tied me up and raped me!"

Whether it was her brother or husband, the young man behind her pulled the woman's head back by her hair and placed a hand over her mouth. "Shut up and let the father finish!"

Father Mark closed his eyes, mumbled what the truck driver took to be a prayer, and then he continued. "We tied Karen to the bed this morning; she was sleeping, fully clothed except for shoes. Her bare feet were covered in dried blood."

The trucker lowered his head to check out the young woman's feet. She was barefoot, and they were stained dark red. When he raised his head to question her, the woman turned from him and stared daggers at the priest.

"When we woke her, we asked where she had been, and where had the blood come from. When she responded with a simple, cold smile, Scott and I both were shaken. Karen's teeth were streaked red.

"I told him that we had to stay strong if we were to save his wife—that we had to stay focused. He agreed, and we approached her again, but we couldn't help ourselves, our eyes were glued to her teeth. When we bent toward her for a closer look, she spit something out of her mouth. Whatever it was landed on her chest. It was fleshy, smooth, and pointed at one end. The other end was ragged. Scott recognized it first and gagged. It was a tongue."

The young woman's chin dropped and she shook her head in disbelief. "How is that even believable? He's saying I kept a tongue in my mouth while I was sleeping? I would have choked! Come on, mister, save me. Get me out of here!"

The priest ignored her and picked up where he left off. "I looked at Karen's eyes—they were bright, shining with delight. I had to turn away. Moments later, I heard a grunt, and I turned back to her. Satisfied that she had our attention, she opened her mouth wide enough for us to see in. Scott groaned. Not only was her tongue still there, but she wiggled it to taunt him. 'Would you like a blowjob, honey?' she asked him. She turned toward me and said, 'Hey Father, guess what? You won't have to listen to that little shit Timmy Williamson's confessions anymore.'"

Karen struggled in the young man's arms and responded angrily. "Who the fuck is Timmy Williamson? You're making all this shit up!"

Father Mark looked up to the heavens and took a deep breath. When he lowered his gaze, he swallowed hard before continuing.

"She got to me. I had no idea if she was telling the truth or not about Timmy, but I believed her. I left the room and walked outdoors to clear my head. I was involved in the cover-up of several crimes, maybe even murder if Karen was telling the truth. I second-guessed my decision to do the exorcism. Though I had committed my help to Scott, I thought about going to the authorities to let them handle the mess. But I understood that would not save Karen. If anything, it would take away any chance she had for salvation. Scott joined me outside. While we were talking, she managed to loosen the restraints and ran from the house. We gave chase and caught up to her here."

The trucker stared at Father Mark. The man's explanation was incredible, yet, he recited it without dramatization. The matter-of-fact manner somehow bolstered his credibility. The truck driver was not a religious man, and he didn't believe in any of that occult crap, but he could see the conviction in the priest's eyes. The trucker shivered at the possibility that Father Mark was telling the truth. He blinked in confusion. His gun hand trembled.

When the young woman laughed, the truck driver swung his gaze to her. Scott had let go of her hair and she had turned her head to him.

"Come on," she giggled, "you can't believe that shit. It sounds like something out of that horror movie where the girl's head spins around. Mister, that's clay on my feet, and my tongue and teeth are fine." She smiled and opened her mouth, exposing a toothy grin. "See, no blood."

If anything, her attempt to prove them wrong had the opposite effect on the truck driver. Her laugh unnerved him. It was cruel. He wanted out of there.

"Okay, you guys. I don't give a rat's ass what you people do to each other up here in New Hampshire. You work this out yourself. I'm leaving."

The trucker backed away from them, not wanting to take his sight off the trio. While the two men followed him with their eyes, the woman took advantage of the distraction. She flung her head back, connecting with Scott's forehead. He grunted and his grip on her loosened. She broke free, turned and punched him in the stomach. As Scott fell to his knees, Father Mark darted forward and wrapped an arm around her neck. He lifted the Bible and pressed it against her cheek. The priest mumbled something the trucker thought might have been Latin, and the woman went limp. He eased her to the ground. Leaving her there, he took a step toward the young man.

"Scott, are you okay?"

"Yeah."

"Good. Please, restrain her while I talk to this man."

Scott bent over the young woman and then sat on her stomach. He reached out and grabbed both of her arms, pinning her to the ground. Father Mark approached the truck driver.

"You know, I never caught your name."

The truck driver's eyes went back and forth between the

couple on the ground and the priest. Settling on Father Mark, the trucker lowered his gun hand. "It's Phil."

"Hey, Phil." Father Mark tucked the Bible under one arm, then he reached inside his black suit coat and pulled out a pack of cigarettes. After tapping the pack and edging one out, he stuck it in his mouth and returned the pack to his coat pocket. He then produced a lighter from his pants pocket. As he lit the cigarette, he managed to say, "I hope you don't mind."

The trucker inched his head back. "Ah, no. They let priests smoke?"

"It's a nasty habit. I've tried to give it up. Now, Phil, what do you have in that trailer that brings you through the armpit of New Hampshire?"

The driver's forehead wrinkled. *Armpit of New Hampshire? Do priests talk like that?* "I was deadheading back from Virginia to Montana, but my dispatch managed to get me a load of computer equipment in Maryland. Then she had me picking up a load up here at the John Deere factory in Stonewall."

Father Mark lifted his head and exhaled a puff of smoke. "John Deere factory? In Stonewall? There's no John Deere factory in Stonewall." He dropped his chin and stared hard into Phil's eyes. "There's only around five hundred people in Stonewall, no factories at all. You've been led astray, Phil." The priest grinned.

The truck driver shook his head. "No, my dispatch gave me the pickup. There's got to be some mistake." *He's lying. Why is he lying?* A voice from the ground interrupted his thoughts.

"When you say dispatch, you mean Nancy?" It was the woman, still pinned beneath Scott.

The truck driver's head turned to her quickly. Ice flowed through his veins. "Y—yes. How do you know her name?"

"I know a lot about Nancy. I know a lot about you, too. I know how both of you have been fucking each other like pigs in the barnyard."

The truck driver's mind clouded over in confusion, and then fear. He was at a loss at how to react. The faces of all three of them were glued to his. He took a step back and raised his gun hand. "How do you know that?"

"You told Nancy that you had had enough, that it was over. You said that you couldn't leave your wife and kids. She was pissed, Phil. Really pissed. Nancy was counting on you to marry her. She's getting even with you. She's going to make your life hell."

Phil stammered, "Y—you mean this is a set-up?"

Scott and Father Mark looked at one another. Scott's lips parted. He was going to say something, but he didn't have the chance. The woman beneath him levitated from the ground, lifting Scott with her. Scott's eyes went wide. When they had risen three feet, their bodies rotated in midair until the woman was on top. She pulled her hands back and broke Scott's grip. Reaching down, the woman grasped his head and squeezed. His screams echoed through the woods. The woman twisted his head to the right, and the trucker heard Scott's neck snap. She continued to twist his head back and forth, until, with a laugh, she yanked on it. The skin of the dead man's neck stretched and then split.

She held his head up and admired her work. When satisfied, she turned toward the priest and lobbed it at him.

The truck driver's heart raced. He pointed the gun at the woman, who was sinking back to the ground. When the two bodies hit the road, she rose and faced him. Her eyes were round, impossibly wide, and entirely white. He tried to back away, but after a step, he hit the front of the cab. His gun arm stretched out straight.

"No!"

The driver turned toward Father Mark.

"Don't shoot her! Karen is still inside!" The priest held out the Bible, pointing it in the woman's direction. "Be gone, demon! Leave this woman and go back to the pit in hell where you belong!"

As he advanced toward her, Father Mark spoke in a language the truck driver couldn't identify, and the young woman went motionless. Her facial skin rippled, and large brown tumors appeared. The flesh on her lips expanded, blowing them out to a grotesque size until they bloodlessly split. Her straight hair turned white, curled, and stood up from her scalp. She pleaded with the priest to stop. She threatened to kill him in horrid ways, and when that did not work, she threatened to kill Karen. All of it fell on deaf ears. Father Mark raised the volume of his chants. When he was close enough to her, he placed the Bible against her head. The smell of burning flesh filled the air and wisps of steam floated above the woman. She went to her knees and the priest followed her down with his Bible. He continued the ritual.

The truck driver grimaced and resisted the urge to vomit, but he never took his eyes off the woman. When she slumped over and became quiet, he hoped whatever the hell had just happened was over. The woman remained on her knees with her chin tight against her chest. Father Mark continued, never wavering in the performance of the ritual. After a few minutes, he became quiet as well. Removing the Bible from her head, he stepped back from the woman. He raised his chin and closed his eyes. His lips moved but the truck driver heard no words.

While Father Mark said his silent prayer, the woman raised her head to him. Etched on her disfigured face was a smile. Her knees straightened, and she slowly stood. The priest's words died in his mouth. He followed her rise with his Bible, pressing it hard against her head, as if he could physically force her back down with it. The trucker noticed no wisps of steam rising from her scalp. He did not smell burning flesh. When Karen stood fully, she turned to the priest. Their faces were inches apart, and then she bent forward until her nose touched his. She laughed. Father Mark didn't move. He closed his eyes and muttered softly, "Our Father, who art in..." He never finished the sentence. The young woman brought her hands up and opened her fingers wide. She reared her elbows back, and then thrust her hands forward, plunging her fingers into Father Mark's stomach. Her hands sunk in to her wrists. The priest gasped, his body shuddered in shock. She lifted him off the ground and held him high above her head. Seconds later, his eyes closed and his body went still. The woman lowered his body to the ground, placed one foot onto his chest for leverage, and then pulled her hands out. She turned to the trucker.

Standing tall, her arms went to her side. Blood flowed over

her hands and down her fingers. The steady drips formed splotches next to her feet. Her milky eyes darted up and down as she studied him. When finished, she cocked her head to the left.

She smiled.

The tumors on her face burst, spraying dark fluid into the air. The woman straightened her head and then laughed with a voice so strained and high-pitched it sounded like a cackle. She reached both hands out to the truck driver.

The trucker fired three shots. All of them hit the woman in the chest. Her body jerked from the impacts, but she remained standing. The volume of her laughter grew as she levitated from the road.

She glided toward him.

The truck driver emptied what was left in the chamber.

It didn't stop her.

She embraced the truck driver.

Wrapping her arms around his waist, she dragged him out into the road. She lifted the trucker's chin until his mouth was even with hers.

In his mind, an image of Karen with her lips pressed against his own faded into black.

"Dispatch. Nancy speaking."

"Hello, Nancy."

"Oh, hey, Phil." Nancy giggled. "How are you enjoying Nowheresville, New Hampshire?"

"I've been thinking, Nancy. I'm going home. I've got some business to take care of with my wife and kids. Then I'm coming for you."

"What? Are you serious?"

"Very."

"Oh, Phil! I can't wait! I love you so much!"

"I'll come for you late this evening."

Nancy cried into the phone. "This is a dream come true. And, Phil, I'm sorry I sent you on that phony pickup. I was angry and hurt. I wasn't thinking right. I know I cost you some money. I promise, I'll make it up to you."

After a long silence, Nancy spoke. "Phil, are you still there?"

"Yes."

"Where are you now?"

"Pennsylvania."

"Okay, I'll see you tonight! I'll keep the bed warm for you. Bye. I love you, Phil!"

A tumor, the size of a golf ball, slid from the center of the truck driver's forehead down to his right cheek. He ended the call without a response.

# STORY NOTES (THE REVEREND'S WIFE)

"*The Reverend's Wife*" is my first, and only, extreme tale.
Gerard Houarner, the author of the acclaimed *Max the Assassin* series of novels and short stories, was putting together an anthology with stories set in his *Painfreak* universe. *Painfreak* is a nightclub where the dead party hard, and those living are lucky to get out alive. He asked if I wanted to contribute to the anthology.

When the first *Max* book appeared, I was stunned by Gerard's literate approach to the horror, despite how raw the action was. We connected on the old Horror World message board and struck up an online friendship. A few years later, when I met Gerard in person at a convention called MoCon, we became even closer. We continued to correspond over the years, and when he gave me a glowing review on my first collection, **The Seeds of Nightmares**, I was overjoyed. Based on **Seeds**, Gerard thought I had the chops to contribute to his new **Painfreak: A Journey of Decadence and Debauchery** anthology (Necro Publications). My first reaction was to ask him if he had the right Tony Tremblay.

I am not an extreme horror writer. While I do include violence in my tales, it is usually to further the story rather than it being a focal point. As for sex, I rarely get graphic. I like to hang in the shadows when it comes to sex and violence, letting the reader imagine what is happening. I explained that I might not be the right guy for this anthology.

I'll never forget Gerard's response. He told me that as an author I should always be stretching out, trying new things. It's the way we grow as writers. His reasoning struck a chord with me. I've tried very hard not to repeat myself, and to explore new narratives and plots. This would be a challenge, and though it scared me a little, I decided to accept it.

I own almost all of Gerard's horror work, including the original "Painfreak" release. I dug it out and reread it along with another related work he published with Tom Piccirilli. I had an idea, and was ready to write.

The plot of "The Reverend's Wife" came somewhat easily, though I cringed while writing most of it. I sent it to Gerard, anticipating the worst. He got back to me shortly after I sent it. I've often thought I should print his reply, frame it, and stick it on the wall in my den. He said, "Tony, your fans are going to hate me."

The story was included in the anthology, and my world didn't fall apart. In fact, I gained some new fans as a result. But that would not be the end of my involvement with Painfreak.

In "The Reverend's Wife", I used a minor character called Rex from a story called "The Pawnshop" which appeared in The Seeds of Nightmares. Rex was promoted to a lead role in "The Reverend's Wife", where he handled his decadence and debauchery like a pro. While I was writing the story, I happened to be working on my first novel, The Moore House. So enamored was I of Rex and the pawnshop owner, I included them in The Moore House. Since Painfreak was fresh in my mind, it was named-checked a few times. I asked Gerard for his permission to use it, and again, his response made me smile. He wrote me back saying he loved it when mythos from two different authors crossed over, and he would be more than happy to let me use Painfreak in my novel.

So, for the hundredth time, I would like to thank Gerard for all the support he has given, and for his greatest gift of all to me...being a brother.

# THE REVEREND'S WIFE

The Reverend Jones touched his index finger to his forehead. He then slipped it to his chest. After a quick tap, he moved it to the left, but stopped midway. For the first time in his life, he was unable to complete the ritual. *Please, God, forgive me.*

He stood before a door that was insanely large for a residence. It was made of steel—the metal tarnished and creased in places. Small, round dents pockmarked the surface. Locks, both keyed and numerical, lined the left side. In the center was a knocker—a simple cast-iron ring—flaked with rust.

Jones beseeched God once more, lifted the knocker, and let it fall. Seconds later, he heard the sound of a bolt sliding. The sound repeated twice more, followed by the *clicks* of locks disengaging. When the door opened, Jones gasped and took a step back. An abomination of a man stood before him.

The largest person he had ever seen took up the width of the doorway. He had to weigh at least 500 pounds. He stood over seven feet tall with scars crisscrossing his face. Bald, his pate reflected the sunlight. He had small black eyes, a flat nose, and his ears stuck out at forty-five-degree angles.

"You Jones?" the giant asked in a guttural voice that was as ugly as his features.

"Y—yes."

"Come."

When the giant man stepped aside, Jones crossed the threshold. As the reverend walked into a living room, the sounds of bolts sliding and locks engaging echoed in his ears. After the giant had finished securing the entrance, he followed Jones in.

"Sit," he grumbled. Jones did as he was told. The giant sat in a love seat opposite him. Jones marveled at the strength of the springs.

"Start talking," the giant commanded.

"It's—it's my wife. She's been missing for two days." Jones expected a reaction, but the giant stared at him without speaking. He swallowed and continued. "She was walking home Tuesday afternoon after getting her hair done when she disappeared. We live in a small apartment behind the Unitarian Church—it's only a fifteen-minute walk from the hairdresser's." He struggled to prevent his voice from cracking. "I went to the police early Tuesday evening when she didn't arrive. They said it was too soon to file a missing person's report so I came back early the next morning. I walked the route with Officer Linson, a member of our church and our friend, to see if we could find anyone who might have seen her. Officer Linson spied a surveillance camera hanging from the Goffstown Pawn Shop, so we went in to see if we could view the footage from the day before. The owner of the shop obliged. When we played the recordings, all three of us saw what happened to my wife." Jones stifled a sob.

The giant nodded for Jones to continue.

"A small person, walking with a crooked gait—it could have been a dwarf—went up to my wife as she was walking home. They spoke for as long as ten minutes. At the end of the conversation, the dwarf pulled out an object. We couldn't identify it after viewing the recording. My wife backed away but he grabbed her hand. He opened it and forced her palm down. He placed the object on top of her hand. My wife must have been in shock because her whole body shook for around five seconds. Then he led her by the hand to the entrance of the brick building they were standing in front of. She didn't resist. They walked in, and then...nothing. We sped up the recording. She never walked out of the building." Jones leaned forward and mumbled a short prayer. When finished, he sat upright.

"The three of us left the pawnshop and rushed over to the brick building. There was no entrance, only a solid wall. We pressed against the bricks and searched for any sign of a hidden doorway, but there was none. All the bricks looked equally weathered, and we saw no fresh mortar. There was an entrance on the right side of the building, but it looked nothing like the one on the recording. We hurried back to the pawnshop to re-watch the recording. Clearly, the entrance was there, as it showed her going in. When we fast-forwarded it to our search of the building, we discovered that the camera had stopped functioning after we had left the pawnshop. There was only snow.

"Officer Linson took the video chip and told us he was headed back to the police station. The pawnshop owner and I went back to the wall to search for anything we might have missed. That's when I saw the card."

The giant raised his head.

"It was wedged in a gap between two bricks where the entrance should have been. Neither of us had seen it earlier. I plucked the card from the wall and it had only one word on it. I was puzzled, so I spoke the word out loud. *Painfreak.*"

If the giant recognized the word, he didn't express it.

"The pawnshop owner asked me to repeat it. When I looked at him, his face was drawn. 'Your wife is in dire straits,' he told me, 'and you have little time to get her back.' I questioned him, begged him to tell me more, but he refused. Instead, he advised me to come see you. He told me your name is Rex and I should bring money." Tears streamed from Jones's eyes. "Can you tell me what's going on, Rex? Can you help me? I'm…"

Rex lifted one of his immense hands, raised its index finger and placed it against his lips. If he didn't hush the reverend, he knew the man would continue jabbering. He needed a few moments to think.

Painfreak. He'd heard rumors of a nightclub called Painfreak, but had always dismissed them. The talk was that its patrons were nightmarish—perversions of humanity—and that it was a sadist's paradise. People said it was vast and was located in a time and space different from ours. The entrance to the club was ever-changing. Nobody knew when or where it would appear. Part of the mythos was that not everyone who entered Painfreak left Painfreak.

Rex was intrigued by the reverend's story. On its surface, it was a far cry from the mundane hit jobs he was used to. As a freelancer, his specialty was government commissions—taking out the scum that the local police or Feds didn't want to bring to trial. He reported to no one, the work paid well, and it provided an opportunity to release his baser instincts without the prospect of incarceration. He loved his work and was known—and feared—for his unique methods of inflicting pain. Working with the government meant periods of feast or famine. When times were slow, Rex would take on outside jobs. These non-government contracts did not hinder his enthusiasm when it came to inflicting pain.

Despite his appearance and line of work, Rex had his principles, and he strictly adhered to them. He abhorred the mistreatment of women, children, and animals, and he harbored compassion for those he deemed innocent or wronged. The Jones woman met at least two of these criteria.

Rex made up his mind—he would talk with the pawnshop owner. He was obliged to thank the man for the reference, but more importantly, he would need more information about Painfreak.

"Two thousand dollars up front, and no guarantees," he croaked." If I bring her back within a week, it will cost you another eight grand. If I can't find her within that time...tough shit."

The reverend reached into his back pocket and removed a billfold. The man opened it and carefully counted out hundred-dollar bills. There were plenty more remaining after the reverend removed twenty of them and handed them over. *I should have asked for more. That's a lot of money for a man of the cloth to possess. Will the heating fund be a little lighter this year, Reverend?*

His hands shaking, the reverend also removed two photographs and placed them beneath the bills. "These are pictures of my wife, Betty. They're fairly recent. My phone number is on the back of one of them."

Rex reached out, took the money and photos. He glanced at the pictures. Betty was mousey—squat, overweight, with her hair brown and cut short to the shoulder. Her heavy breasts sagged to the bottom of her rib cage. Her face was neither attractive nor ugly, with no distinguishing features. Rex placed the photos and money on a small table next to the loveseat. After a brief silence, both men stood. Rex pointed to the front door and the reverend, with his head lowered, walked toward it. *Feeling guilty about the money?* After he unlocked the door and threw the slide-bolts, he opened it and the reverend passed through. "I'll be in touch," he grunted.

The reverend didn't look back.

Sixteen hours had passed since the reverend had paid him a visit. It was now dark enough for Rex to travel. In daylight it was impossible for him to avoid the stares and horrified reactions of people. He climbed into his Hummer and drove to the pawnshop. The owner must have expected him, as he could see bright light streaming from the gap between the front double doors.

Much like Rex, the pawnshop owner was an enigma to the townspeople. The owner was seldom seen in the shops or restaurants, and he never advertised. If someone wandered into the shop in pursuit of second-hand goods, they always left disappointed. The only wares on the shelves were esoteric artworks, foreign language books, and mechanical contraptions that defied simple description. If any would-be customer lingered too long, the owner simply mentioned how costly the items were and that was usually enough to goad most of them to leave. If that didn't work, he had other ways. The word on the street was the owner was an occult practitioner and Rex knew this to be true. The pawnshop owner had approached him over the years for assistance, and Rex saw firsthand the methods he had used.

Rex parked his Hummer a block away and walked back to the pawnshop. Seeing the doors were unlocked, he opened them all the way. With a little effort, he pushed his girth through. Inside, he ignored the shelves of goods and proceeded to a long counter in front of the left wall. The pawnshop owner stood there with a frown, his arms crossed over his chest.

"Good evening, Rex."

"Evening. Thank you for the reference." His voice sounded like a car driving over gravel.

"You're here, so I assume you took the job. This is going to be a bad one, Rex. No one who goes into Painfreak comes out quite the same—if they come out at all."

Rex cleared his throat and growled, "Can you get me in?"

"I think so. Stand on the sidewalk in front of the brick building across the street."

"Now?"

"You don't have much time, as it might already be too late. If I can bring the entrance back, I'm not sure I can hold it here for too long after you go inside. You get in, Rex, and then you get out as soon as you can."

"What happens if I don't?"

"You might still be able to leave. I just don't know where to."

Rex knew this job could be the biggest mistake of his life, but the lure of Painfreak, with its rumors of sexual abandon and unfettered carnage was too deep to ignore. He had to see this place. "Let's do this."

Every passing car slowed. The occupants' eyes widened and their heart rates accelerated when they caught a glimpse of what stood on the sidewalk across the street from the pawnshop. Their headlights revealed a giant—as big as or bigger than any pro wrestler or comic book movie character they had ever seen—standing still, his gaze set on the bricks before him. If he turned his head and the angle was right, they could see his face. Engines were gunned, some cars leaving rubber in their wake.

Except for an occasional sweep of his head left or right, Rex stared at the brick wall for maybe an hour. Fatigued, he closed his eyes for a moment. When he reopened them, the entrance to Painfreak filled his vision. He breathed deeply, and before he could step toward it, he felt a pull on his pant leg. He looked down and saw a little man bent at the waist. The reverend's assumption was correct—it was a dwarf.

"Hey there, big fella," the dwarf squeaked, "you want to go someplace where your wildest sexual fantasies come true?"

Rex raised an eyebrow and stared at the little man.

The dwarf continued in his helium-high voice. "Big guy like you, hell, you would fit right in! We got girls. We got small girls with big tits and big girls with small tits. We got boys, too, if you want. You like boys? We got big boys with small dicks and small boys with big dicks. We got other things, too. Things you never dreamed of...and maybe some you have."

While Rex's mind went to images of things he had dreamed of, the dwarf removed a metallic object from his pants pocket.

"Ahh," squealed the dwarf as he spotted the massive erection forming in Rex's pants. He held up the object. "Your admission. You'll have to bend over a bit and give me your right hand, big fella."

Rex obeyed, and the dwarf pressed the object to the top of Rex's wrist. Electricity flowed through his arm. It dissipated before it reached his elbow. The dwarf pocketed the metal object. "Big guy like you, you hardly felt that, I bet. Let's go!" he announced in a voice that brought to Rex's mind fingernails on a chalkboard.

Together, they passed through the doorway, where they were met by a tall, thin Asian man. "Your right hand," the Asian demanded. Rex held it out, palm down. The Asian waved a wand over his hand. Rex cocked his head when a symbol resembling a bone came into view. The Asian nodded and then gestured with a sweep of his arm toward a hallway leading into the club.

Rex looked down to his side to see if the dwarf would follow, but he was gone. He eyed the hallway, pitch black and as quiet as a mausoleum. He stepped forward.

"Welcome to Painfreak."

Rex jumped, then crouched at the sound. The dwarf's voice had come from somewhere above him.

After no more than three steps down the hallway, Rex's senses were assaulted. Dance music enveloped him, the vibration digging its way through his pores. He cringed, the pain from the booming audio traveling through his ears and piercing his brain. The down-beat was worse—it pricked at his eyes like needles while the bass jackhammered the top of his skull. Why hadn't he heard it when he was wrist-checked by the Asian?

*This is Painfreak? A dance club?*

Rex compartmentalized the pain. He concentrated on his surroundings. Hundreds of people were dancing under strobe lights, their bodies vanishing and then reappearing in time with the rhythm. The flashes disoriented him and he fought to maintain focus.

A majority of the dancers were nude or semi-nude. Breasts and penises bounced, the flaccid ones lagging behind the beat. Of those clothed, some were wearing costumes and masks.

The smell of fish and bleach permeated the air.

Rex advanced toward the center of the dance floor and bull-dozed anyone in his path to the side. No one seemed to care. Those who fell reached out to him. Their hands snaked up his legs. When they reached for his cock, he ignored them or brushed them aside with his tree-trunk arms. Some of the fallen ones would not be deterred—they clung to his legs. He dragged them along. Some fell off, others he stepped on. If they cried out, he didn't hear their wails.

Rex pushed on. His gaze swept over the costumes of the dancers. Both sexes wore bras adorned with metallic accoutre-ments. Woven into the fabric were spikes, fragments of saw blades, and razor wire. The objects glistened with moisture when the strobe lights reflected off them. He had no way of knowing what lay beneath their masks, but a grin formed when he imagined that they might be more hideous than he was. He reached out to pull the mask off the closest dancer, but stopped short when there was a tap in the middle of his back. With his arm suspended in air, he turned. When he saw who it was, he took an involuntary step away.

It was Brian Stone. Only, Brian Stone was dead. Rex knew this because he had killed him.

Two years ago Stone bludgeoned his wife with a hammer and then had stuck the handle up her ass. She bled to death. Stone claimed he found her that night when he came home from playing poker with some pals. He told the cops she was cheat-ing on him, and that's who they should be looking for. Everyone knew he did it, but the cops couldn't crack his alibi or get enough evidence. They wanted Stone to disappear. When the detectives showed Rex the pictures of Stone's wife lying on the floor, dead, with the handle sticking out of her, Rex was only too happy to accept the job. He beat Stone to a pulp—repeatedly slamming his fists into the man's face until a portion of the prick's skull broke off. The sidewalk was still stained where his brains had spilled.

Now, Stone showed no sign of the beating.

Rex's chest tightened. Not in fear of the dead man—for Rex feared no one—but because the images of what Stone had done to his wife rushed at him like a chained dog.

Stone must have noted the recognition in Rex's eyes. The dead man smiled, and then motioned with a shake of his head for Rex to follow. Rex weighed the invitation. Without waiting, Stone turned and exited the dance floor. Unlike his own entrance into the club, the crowd parted for Stone. Rex decided to follow. They passed a long bar against a far wall, two people deep with customers ordering drinks. Stone turned at the bar's end and opened an oversized door. Rex entered, and when Stone closed the door behind them, the music cut out.

They were in a small, well-lit room, facing each other with only a few feet separating them. Another oversized door loomed at the opposite end.

Rex grunted, "You're dead."

"Yes, I'm dead. Only, in Painfreak, I'm not dead."

Rex cocked his head to the side. *How can someone be dead but not dead?*

Stone continued. "We know why you are here. She's in a room through that door." Stone lifted a hand and pointed. "Before you open the door, Rex, I'm here to tell you that Painfreak thinks you are making a mistake. She belongs here. And so do you."

Stone's words only fueled Rex's hatred for the man. Nobody told him what he should or shouldn't do, especially a woman-beating shit-heel like Stone. *What kind of place brings people like Stone back from the dead?* Rex balled his hands into fists. One of the pictures the detectives had shown him flashed in his head. He saw the hammer Stone had used to kill his wife. Clumps of flesh, painted red and brown, clung to the handle.

Rex howled at the image and lifted his arms high. Stone's eyes went wide and he leaned back.

The giant brought his arms down.

Tuffs of hair and bone fragments exploded from Stone's head. Rex continued to pummel the once-dead man until his neck vertebrae wedged deep in his upper torso. Stone teetered for a moment, and then toppled over sideways.

"Fucking stay dead," Rex mumbled.

He turned from Stone's body, walked to the door on the other side of the room, opened it, and stepped through.

In the center of the small room hung a naked woman. She was bound with rope and suspended upright. Her stretched arms and legs formed an X. Four men surrounded her. They were thin, bald, with skin as pale as a cancer patient. One was positioned behind her, another faced her so close their noses touched. A third man rubbed against the woman's left thigh. The fourth man stood next to the woman's right thigh with a knife. The man drew the blade across the meaty portion of the woman's thigh. With his fingers, he parted her flesh until the blood flowed freely. Then the man plunged his penis into the wound. Rex squinted and shook his head as he stared at the man.

He gazed at each of the pale men. They all pumped into the woman, their asses in constant, rapid motion. The woman's body had too many cuts for Rex to count, all of them dripping with blood and semen.

Rex lifted his head to see their victim's face. Her eyes were tight, and her mouth was open. Her tongue hung limp over her bottom lip. It was the reverend's wife. He strained to hear if she was aware of what was happening to her, then he heard it—a single, continuous, anguished note coming from somewhere deep inside her.

He walked toward the men fucking her.

Rex couldn't remember a time when he had wept. Even as a child he had kept his emotions in check. He took a deep breath, hung his head and closed his eyes. His shoulders sagged as he exhaled. His eyes moistened. Scenes of his mother's torture by her boyfriend seeped into his head. Rex saw himself as a child, forced to witness the depravity. He tensed at the recollection. His hands opened and then closed into fists.

Now was not the time to revisit those memories. He blocked out the images, and his mind raced to the present. When he opened his eyes, they burned with fire.

Hands the size of melons gripped the biceps of the pale man closest to him. Rex squeezed. The man's bones crushed under his grip. With little effort, he tore the man's arms out of their sockets.

The man continued to pump into the woman.

Rex blinked and took a step back. *What the fuck?* Rex dropped the man's limbs, reached out, and wrapped his fingers around the man's neck. He pulled. The head separated from the body. Blood sprayed, adding another layer of gore to Rex's face and chest.

It wasn't enough. Rex fumed. *Why the fuck won't he die?*

Rex pulled the man out of the woman and onto the floor. His size twenty-two shoes stomped on the body until it was a bloody sludge. Piles of viscera mixed with bones littered the floor. They did not move. Rex turned to the other three. They had paid no attention to the death of one of their own. If anything, their assault on the woman grew more fevered. Rex tore into them. One by one, he repeated the tactic on the remaining three. When finished, his pant legs were soaked red to the knees.

Rex surveyed the carnage. What could have passed for a smile stretched across his face.

The woman groaned. It brought Rex back to the reason he was here. Had he had time, he would have bathed in the blood and devoured their organs, but he had a job to do and he wasn't sure how much longer he could remain in Painfreak before he was trapped. He searched the floor for the knife the men had used to cut her, but he couldn't find it. Using the toe of his right shoe, he moved the piles of sludge aside for a better view. The knife revealed itself under a mashed organ. As he bent to pick it up, he heard a sound above him. He lifted his head and frowned. There was no ceiling. In its place was a dark void. As he stared, he saw something move within it. Seconds later, an object, attached to a thin white rope, slipped down through the ink. When it touched the floor several feet away, Rex stood upright, the knife clenched in his hand.

It was a woman—naked, tall, hairless, and as pale as the four men he had killed. The thin white rope hung slack as it stretched down from the void and disappeared behind her back. A web of sorts, he mused, no doubt spun from her ass. She stood still for a moment, then stepped forward, closing the distance between them.

"Rex," she spoke, her voice low and thick. "You do not want to take her away."

He took a step back, and bumped up against the woman bound by ropes. She groaned, but then went silent.

Rex eyed the pale woman—not so much in fear but out of curiosity. "Why not?"

The woman had come to within inches of Rex. She stopped, raised her arms, and then wrapped them around Rex's head. "Because, Rex..." Her lips didn't move, but he could hear her voice. "...you may leave Painfreak, but Painfreak never leaves you." She raised her head and then pressed her mouth against his. Her lips parted and her tongue probed.

Rex stiffened. His body vibrated as if four hundred and sixty volts of electricity poured through him. Pictures played in his head. They were scenes of exquisite debauchery, and he had the lead role in all of them. Rex could taste blood, and he could smell his victim's shit. He saw himself surrounded by women, all of them offering themselves to him, their sexes dripping with anticipation. Above it all, a whisper called to him. It was the pale woman's, her voice breathy as she implored, "Stay with us."

*Stay with us.*

*Us?*

Rex bit down on the woman's tongue. In his head he heard her shriek, and the images of the debauchery vanished. She lowered her hands and pushed off him. Blood bubbled from between her lips. Rex shook off the remnants of her psychic hold and spit the severed tongue back at her. The thin white rope pulled taut and she was lifted into the darkness. As he watched her rise, he raised his fists to her and growled, "Us? There is no *Us*! Nobody owns me!"

He turned to the trussed woman. Starting with her leg restraints, he cut them, and worked up to the ties that bound her arms. He slung her over his shoulder.

"No," she pleaded.

"Shut up," he answered, "I've got you now. I'm taking you home to your husband."

Rex retraced his steps. He waded through the piles of mashed organs on the floor and opened the door.

Walking through the room, he glanced at the mess that was Stone. *Still dead.* He exited that room and was back at the bar on the dance floor. The music drove spikes of pain into his head and the strobe lights played havoc with his perspective. He searched for the way he had entered. Taking a few moments to adjust to the lights, he thought he had found it. As before, the crowd clamored for him. They reached out, grabbed at his legs, and ran their hands over his body. A few attempted to remove the woman from his shoulder. He answered with a punch that snapped their limbs or stove in their skulls. He barreled his way through the dance floor, kicking, pushing, and stepping on anyone in his path. When he made it to the end of the room, he saw the dark hallway. He stopped before entering and turned to take one last look at Painfreak. Though the music droned on and the strobe lights continued flashing, no one in the crowd danced. They were still, and they all faced him. When the strobe lights flashed on, he saw their grinning faces. His headed clouded. They were pulling at him. Once more it was the woman on his shoulders who brought him back around.

"Leave me alone," she begged. She was disoriented, her voice weak. Rex ignored her, blinked at the mob, and then he spun around. He walked into the hallway.

The music stopped and the lightning bolt echoes from the strobes disappeared. There were no signs of the Asian man or the dwarf. Rex walked to the door at the end of the hallway, opened it and stepped outside.

It was dark, but the surroundings were familiar. He stood in front of the brick building and could see the pawnshop across the street. Its lights were off. He carried the woman to his Hummer and drove home.

Rex entered the house, carried the woman up to the second floor, and placed her on his bed. She was conscious, her eyes fixed on his. Neither said a word. His gaze wandered over her body, her wounds trickling red and white onto his blankets—except from between her legs. There, a puddle formed beneath her. A snapshot of the men fucking her flashed before him. He saw her bound, the knife cutting her thigh, their frantic pumping.

Rex envied their single-minded purpose.

"Why did you take me from there?"

He lifted his gaze in response to Betty's question. His hoarse reply came quick. "Your husband. He paid me to bring you back."

Betty arched her back and spread her legs wide. "I don't want to come back."

Rex focused on the gap between her legs. Betty was small, too small. He would rip her apart.

After a moment, he murmured, "There's something I have to do."

Rex pulled Betty's picture from his pocket. He walked to the phone and dialed the number on the back. After three rings someone answered.

"Reverend, I've got Betty. Come over in an hour, not before. The front door is unlocked, let yourself in." Rex hung up the phone. He disrobed and approached the bed.

"We are going to have company soon."

Betty grinned. "I can't wait."

# STORY NOTES (TROUT FISHING AT GLEN LAKE)

*After the release of my novel* The Moore House, *I was flattered by how much attention one of the characters received. People wanted to know more about the mysterious owner of the pawnshop. I admit to liking the character quite a bit myself.*

*Though I usually do not have an idea in mind when I set out to write a short story, I knew I wanted to write another one that included the pawnshop owner. A title came to me—"Trout Fishing at Glen Lake" (Glen Lake is an actual lake located in my hometown, Goffstown), and after typing it, the plot almost wrote itself. Writing stories is hard work. It takes me months to get them right as I am constantly editing and rewriting them. "Trout Fishing at Glen Lake" did take me months to write, but I enjoyed every minute of it.*

*When I finished the tale, I sent it to a few friends to see what they thought of it. My dear friend, Nanci Kalanta, wrote me back saying it was the best thing I had ever written. Talk about pumping someone up!*

*I sent it out to a professional and well-respected anthology call, and the editor raved over it. Emails went back and forth telling me how great the story was, how it needed very few edits, and to thank me for sending them a "kick-ass" story. Then, out of nowhere, it was rejected. No explanation was offered. I was heartbroken.*

*Thinking there was something amiss with the story, I sent it to my editing company of choice and asked them why they thought it was rejected. They didn't understand why it wasn't accepted (especially after the initial raves it received). They thought it was very good, but they did suggest I edit out a few lines that did not serve the tale. I made the corrections, but held off in sending it out again.*

*"Trout Fishing at Glen Lake" makes its publishing debut here. If you get a chance after reading it, let me know what you think.*

# TROUT FISHING AT GLEN LAKE

I think September is the best time for trout fishing. Trout are more likely to take the bait when the water is cold. Unfortunately, the beginning of September is when fishing season ends. It's also when school starts.

I'm a sophomore at Goffstown High this year. There are only twenty-five kids in my class, and I've been sharing homerooms with almost all of them since I was seven. It makes me smile when I think about how I used to grab at Vivian Auclair's hair to tease her—now I grab something else of hers. She's my girlfriend and I'm gonna live with her someday, though she keeps telling me to hold my horses.

Viv can't spend time with me today, so I grab my pole and tackle box. I plan on doing a little solo fishing at Devil's Rock. It's about half a mile down one of the trails into the woods. It's at the start of that trail where I see John.

John's family moved up here from Haverhill, Massachusetts, last spring. He hasn't made a lot of friends yet, but from what little time I spent with him in class and in gym, he seems to be an okay guy.

"Hey, John! What's up?"

Phone in hand, John headed up the trail. He has his earbuds in and I guess he doesn't hear me. I wave my pole to catch his attention. He notices me and pops the earbuds out. I ask him again.

"Nothing, Billy." John wasn't much of a talker.

"Oh." Not that I'm much of one either.

We both look around. Like me, I'm sure he's pretending the scenery has something to catch his interest, but that lasts about ten seconds. I decide I have to say something at the risk of straining my neck.

"I'm going fishing. Want to come?"

John's eyes brighten. "Sure."

He pockets his phone and earbuds and walks beside me on the path. John and I don't say much while we make our way. I ask if he fishes. He says he never has. I tell him that next spring I'll let him borrow my extra pole. He says thanks. Neither of us minds the lack of conversation, though. It feels natural being out in the woods. When we come to the spot in the trail where we have to veer off, I point with the pole and we turn onto a narrower path, full of crabgrass. We walk along it until I see the lake and the huge boulder I call Devil's Rock. I hold out my arm to slow John.

"Okay," I say in a hushed voice, "we need to stay quiet."

John scrunches his face. "Why?"

"'Cause I don't want the fish to hear us."

He snorts. "Fish don't have ears."

"Maybe, maybe not. What I do know is that if we're too loud, they'll know we're coming."

After a moment, he shrugs and nods.

I've come here so many times I could probably get to it blind-folded, but I slow down to make sure John doesn't trip over a root or get whacked in the face by a branch. The area around the base of the boulder is bare, trodden down from all the people fishing here. When we get to the rock, I put my hand in front of John again. We both stop. I cock an ear to the lake.

"Do you hear something?" I ask.

John tilts his head and listens. "Yeah, I do. It sounds like people talking."

We walk lightly and go around to the side of the rock where the voices are coming from.

About a hundred feet down shore, there are three men in a small clearing. They're to the right of us, which means we must have passed them on the trail walking in. Two of the men are standing, and the third is on his knees, facing the water, his back to his companions. The men standing are dressed in black suits, white shirts, and black shoes. Their hair is cut short—I can see their ears from here. The man kneeling is also wearing a white shirt. It has large red stains on it. I lower the fishing pole and tackle box to the ground and push John back behind the rock. Our eyes are wide and we aren't sure what to do. We lean in closer and listen.

"Please, don't. I have a family."

"You should have paid Sullivan the money then."

"I will this time, I promise!"

John's mouth opens and my chin drops. I recognize one of the voices. It's Mr. Day, our gym teacher. We hunker close to the ground and inch our heads around the rock. We have a good view, and despite the kneeling man's wailing and head shaking, I confirm it *is* Mr. Day.

One of the men in black, taller than the other, replies to Mr. Day.

"You've promised us way too many times before, Bob."

The tall man nods to his partner. The shorter guy lifts his arm—he's holding a gun. He steps forward and places it against the back of Mr. Day's head. A second later, we hear a muffled pop. The top of Mr. Day's head flies off into the lake. His body wavers for a few moments, and then collapses forward, face-down into the water.

"*Holy shit!*" John cries.

My face goes blank for a second, and then I turn to look at John. Shaking, he turns to meet my gaze. The palm of his hand covers his mouth.

We stare at each other for a second, then peer back at the men.

They are looking our way.

"B-Billy, I'm—I'm sorry."

I twist around and grab John's head with both hands. "Shhh. Be quiet!"

John nods and we chance another look at the men.

They're not there.

By the time I yell "*Run*," I'm a step ahead of him.

My heart has never beaten so fast in my life. I want to pick up speed, but the path is too narrow and the overhanging brush slows me down. I can't focus more than a few feet ahead because the ground is uneven and there's a risk of turning my ankle. Twice I feel my foot slip, but both times, I manage to shift my weight and avoid twisting it. Any thought of dodging branches while I'm flying down the path is long gone. I don't even think to make sure the ones I push aside don't whack John on the head when they swing back. I keep my ears open, though, making sure he's behind me. As long as I can hear his footsteps and heavy breathing, I know he's there.

Our ten-minute walk from the main trail to the rock takes us less than half that to get back. Instead of taking a left, which would lead us to those men, I take a sharp right shouting, "This way!" The thud of John's sneakers hitting the dirt behind me is all the reply I need.

Though I'm running as fast as I can now that we're on the main trail, John catches up. We're side by side, shooting up the path like scared deer running from wild dogs.

"Where we going?" he asks between breaths.

"Around that bend, up there, is another path," I reply, pointing and gasping. "A side path to an old storage building." I wait a few breaths before going on. "That storage building is on Church Street. We can follow Church Street into town."

"You think they're following us?"

I turn to him, and he looks back at me. "Yeah," I say between chest hitches. "I think they're coming for us." John's eyes go wide and his face tightens. Next thing I know he's ahead of me.

The urge to slow down and check for those men is fierce, but the path leading to the storage building is coming up; a quick turn of my head when we round it should satisfy that impulse.

"That rock ahead," I shout. "Turn onto the path after that!" John makes it to the boulder, but as he slows for the turn, I hear a sound. John's back straightens. His head flies up and he seems to get a few inches taller. He collapses at the foot of the path.

I stop at the rock, turn to look back, and I see them: the two men. One is standing, but he's not moving. The other has one knee on the ground with his arms out straight, a gun pointed at us.

I lean over and pull John behind the rock. I let go of him—and one of my hands is covered in blood. Turning him over, there's a dark spot on his back, near his left shoulder. The area around it is turning a deep red, and it's growing larger.

"John, can you run?"

"Not sure. I can try." I can barely hear him; his voice is so soft.

I wrap my arm around his good shoulder and lift him to his feet. "Lean on me—the building is only fifty feet away. Come on man, we gotta do this."

John nods, and together we head down the path. He doesn't last long before he falls limp against me. I don't have time to explain to him what I'm going to do. I lift him, throwing him over my shoulder. I brace him as best I can, then take off.

The small man shot John from about a hundred and fifty feet away. If they stop at the beginning of this path and fire again, we'll be sitting ducks. With John over my shoulder, he would take the bullet. I'm ashamed for thinking this, but I know it's my only hope if they catch up to us.

I run as fast as I can. John slips, but I push him back square on my shoulder. My legs ache like crazy, and I'm breathing so hard, I worry I won't catch any air. I see the end of the path, and beyond it the storage building on Church Street. A few feet in front of me, a small patch of dirt and twigs explodes off the ground. I run past, and it happens again. That's all I need to spur me on.

I burst out of the woods and take a sharp left to the building. There are two large swinging doors at the rear, but they're closed, an oversized lock hanging between them. I keep moving. When I reach the front corner of the building, I round it, and come to a dead stop. *What the heck?* The front of the building is different from what I remember, and I saw it only two days ago.

It used to look the same as the back of the building, the only difference being small windows on either side of the wooden doors. Now, enormous tinted glass windows line the front. Farther down in this sea of windows is a set of double glass doors sitting in the middle.

I need to make a decision. Do I waste more time here to see if someone's inside, or do I make a run for it down Church Street?

I'm sure I won't get far carrying John. I look up. The new owners put an awning up over the doors. There is an inscription on it. In big black block letters, it reads GOFFSTOWN PAWNSHOP. What are the odds of a pawnshop being open on a Sunday? I rush to the doors to find out. I push, they open, and I charge through.

"Help," I shout, "*Help!*" The doors swing shut and I lean back against them. John moans and I lower him to the floor.

"What brings you into my establishment, young man?"

I can't tell where the voice is coming from. Except for racks full of stuff lining the walls, the pawnshop is empty. To my left, a counter runs almost the entire length of the wall. I follow it with my eyes, and that's when I see him, standing at the far end of the counter. He's a tall, thin man, and despite the distance, I can see his eyes. They are bright gray, gleaming like polished steel. From the way he is staring, I swear he can see inside me.

"Please, mister, you've got to help us. These two guys are after us, and they shot—"

Bolts of lightning strike the back of my head. I pitch headfirst toward the floor. My nose hits the cement, crushing the cartilage and adding to my agony. My forehead makes contact a split second later. For the first time in my life, I know what it means when people say they saw stars. The pawnshop is getting fuzzy, fading to black.

I'm about to pass out, but a blow to my ribs turns the lights back on. I crawl forward a few feet to escape more pain. Moaning, I stop and struggle to turn over. I squint through my haze toward the front doors.

The two men have followed us in. The taller one stands by the doors and stares at something outside. He calls out, "A cable company truck pulled up across the street. Looks like we have to hang tight for a while."

The other man nods. He hovers over me but his gaze is elsewhere—he's staring at the guy at the end of the counter and pointing a gun at him. Without taking his eyes off the guy, the short man says to me, "Get up, or I'll kick you again."

Every muscle in my body protests as I pick myself up off the floor. The room spins a little when I stand, so I focus on a spot on the wall to make it stop. My eyes land on the top shelf of a rack. There's a picture frame there, and what looks like a metal box behind it. The frame appears to hold a modern art painting. I stare at it for a few moments and the room stops spinning. My gaze wanders to the door and I see John, spread-eagle on the floor.

*John!*

I'm wide awake now and take a few steps toward him. The shorter man swivels and points his gun at me.

"Look," I tell him, "I just want to help my friend. Please?"

The man looks to his partner, who nods. The tall man then turns to the guy at the counter and asks, "Hey, how do you lock these doors?"

I bend down to John. He's moaning and there's a pool of blood underneath him. I look up to the tall man. "He's bleeding bad. He needs help."

He looks to the guy at the end of the counter and says, "After you tell me how to lock these doors, help the kid with his friend."

The guy at the counter doesn't say anything; he doesn't even move. He stares at the tall man so hard it makes me uncomfortable. I have to say something. "Come on, mister. Please?"

The tall man reaches into his suit coat and pulls out a gun. He aims it at John. "You've got five seconds to answer me."

The guy at the counter remains silent.

The tall man leans forward and raises the gun until it's aimed at John's head.

"Please, mister!" I beg.

A reply finally comes and the guy points at the counter. "Okay. I have a switch—a button. When I press it, the doors will lock."

"Does that button also call the cops?"

"No." I could swear the corners of his lips turn up slightly when he answers. The tall man must not have seen it because he hurries over to where the guy pointed. He scans the counter. "Is this the button?"

The guy nods.

"Then get over here and press it."

The guy moves to that end of the counter, but before he can get behind it, the tall man says, "Nope, you stay on this side."

If I had doubts that the corners of the guy's lips curled up a moment ago, there's no question they drop when he's told to remain on this side of the counter. He hesitates, and I can almost see the gears turning in his head. But it doesn't take him long to sort out what's going through his mind. His face returns to its steely expression, and the guy walks to the center of the counter.

"Remember," the tall man cautions. "No police."

"Oh," comes a reply, "I guarantee there will be no police."

The guy reaches over to the counter and presses the button.

I'm not sure what to expect. In spite of the guy's comment, I thought for sure that after he pressed the button, red lights would flash, a siren would wail, or steel bars would drop from the ceiling to cover the doors and windows. Instead, all I hear is a *thunk*. It's loud, though, and I catch its echo at the far end of the shop.

The tall man jiggles the door handle. "All right, help the kid if you want."

The guy walks over to me and John, taking charge right away. "We're going to lift him up and place him on the counter. What's your name, son?"

"Billy."

"Okay, Billy, grab his legs; I'll take the arms. On the count of three, we lift and put him there." He motions with his head to a space on the counter. "One—two—three!"

Because John isn't heavy, we manage to move him with little effort. We place him on the counter with his bad shoulder facing the wall. The guy goes to work on John as soon as we put him down.

"Are you the owner of this place?" I ask.

"Yes," he replies without slowing down.

"When did you move here?"

"The shop moves around a lot." What might have passed for a smile crosses his lips. After he removes my friend's shirt, he inspects the wound.

"Hey!" It's the short man. He is over by the racks on the

far wall—picking up, looking over, and then replacing va items. "What kind of place is this?"

The guy replies without turning his head. "It's a pawnshc Didn't you read the awning?"

"Doesn't look like any kind of pawnshop I've ever seen. This is some weird-looking shit."

The pawnshop owner bunches up John's shirt and hands it to me. "Billy, press this over the hole. Hold it tight. We need to keep the blood from flowing out. The wound looks worse than it is. It's nothing that can't be taken care of if we get him help soon." As I take the shirt, he turns to face the short man.

"I have a discerning clientele. They don't walk in off the street. Almost all of my business is done by other means."

"You mean like the Internet?"

"Yes … and word of mouth."

The tall man is quiet while everyone talks, staying by the doors and looking out the windows. His gun remains drawn, and he holds it close to his chest.

"Hey, what's this?" The short man holds up a rectangular black box. From what I can see, it's almost two feet long and about a foot square. At its end a round hole in the center takes up half the space.

The pawnshop owner's eyes brighten. It's the first time since we burst into his place that he's had a full-on smile. "That's a *faience* box!" He answers in a tone that has a hint of admiration in it. "It's two thousand years old—a relic of the Kush kingdom in Sudan. King Amanitore himself commissioned that box as a testament to his royal power. The faience boxes of the era were usually manufactured to assist those in the afterlife. The one you are holding, however, is different. Not only is it lacking the traditional depiction of a set of eyes that warded off evil spirits, it's devoid of color. As you can see, it's entirely black. It also differs in its purpose."

The short man's eyes widen. "No shit! It's two thousand years old, huh?" He calls to his partner at the door. "Hey Randy, this must be worth a fortune! Mr. Sullivan would love this, I bet."

Fury burns in the tall man's eyes, and I think I know why.

We now know his name is Randy, and his boss's name is Mr. Sullivan. This isn't good. My hands shake while I apply pressure to John's wound. The short man is oblivious to his mistake, which also can't be good for us.

"What's its purpose?" the short man asks.

"The records made it quite clear that it was a loyalty device. It was common in those days for a king to be deposed, usually by family members. As a way to thwart assassination, the king instructed his holy men to infuse the box with the ability to make an assessment on those who would succeed him. When the king died, his soul would transfer into that box. His would-be successor would be required to place their arm inside. The king would pass judgment on him from the afterlife."

The short man's eyes squint. "What do you mean?"

The pawnshop owner sighs. "It means if the soul of the king decided his would-be successor would govern the kingdom with a steady hand and a pure heart, the king would imbue the man with special gifts."

"Special gifts? Like what?"

The pawnshop owner shakes his head. "We don't know for sure—the records on this particular faience box didn't say. Other boxes were said to impart the ability to foreshadow and to grant the power of invisibility."

"Foreshadow? What does that mean?"

Heck, even I know what that means. But if the pawnshop owner is put off by the short man's ignorance, he doesn't show it. He answers the question without looking irritated. "It means he could see the future."

The short man is delighted by the answer. "Wow! What a lucky bastard that guy would be! He'd know who was coming for him, turn invisible, and kill them."

He brings the box over to the counter, placing it on top, the hole facing him.

I have to admit I'm also caught up in the story, but there is one important piece of information the short man didn't ask for. I was about to ask it myself, but as I open my mouth, the pawnshop owner shoots me a glare so fierce I shut up right away.

The short man places his gun on the counter and then pulls

the left sleeve on his suitcoat up as high as it will go, bunching it up around his elbow. He unbuttons his shirt sleeve and rolls that up to his elbow, too. As I watch the short man stick his arm out and wiggle his fingers, it dawns on me why the pawnshop owner glared at me. It looks as if I'm about to get my answer without even having to ask the question.

"Hey, Randy," the short man sticks his hand into the box and says between chuckles, "watch me turn invisible."

I can't help myself—I lean closer to see what happens.

But nothing does.

The short man stares at the box. He doesn't say anything, but I can tell from the way the corners of his mouth dip that he's disappointed. Looking toward Randy, he shrugs and laughs.

His left shoulder jerks. It jerks again and the box slides toward him a few inches. He struggles, like he's trying to pull his arm out, but he can't. After a few more tugs, he holds the box down with his free hand, and tries again.

"Hey, asshole," he says, "I can't get my hand out of this thing."

Randy shakes his head. He looks at the pawnshop owner. "Can you help him get his hand out of that box?" The way he says it doesn't sound like a question, though—more like when my mom is pissed and wants me to do something without yelling at me.

The pawnshop owner faces Randy, staring at him. "No," the pawnshop owner says, "I can't. King Amanitore is passing judgment."

The short man's eyes go wide. His voice rises. "What? What the hell are you talking about? Get me out of this—ahhhhhh!"

All three of us stare at the short man. His screams bounce off the walls and his body shakes so much it looks as if he's plugged into a power outlet. Blood pours from his eyes, spraying the counter and floor in weird patterns. He opens his mouth and chokes out dark clots that collect on his chest. I gasp as his legs lift from the floor. They arc out to the side, rising until his body is horizontal with the box. Blood pools on the floor beneath him.

"Make it stop!" Randy shouts. "Get it to stop!"

The pawnshop owner replies, "I can't."

Randy rushes to the counter and places the tip of his gun against John's forehead. "You better find a way. Do it now!"

With a slow shake of his head, the pawnshop owner repeats his answer. "I can't."

*Click—bang*! A second later, my face is covered in blood.

The top of John's skull and the upper portion of his face are gone. Some of his brain drips down into a cavity above his mouth, settling in a dark soup of red with bits of white fragments that poke through the surface.

The tension in my arms drains. I let go of the shirt I was pressing against John's shoulder.

This can't be real. None of this can be happening. I must be at home, tired and confused, watching a movie, maybe.

The view around me recedes. I'm elevated, looking down at all of us. John looks so small from up here. I turn away from my dead friend and see the owner staring at him. There is a man with a gun standing close to me, and I know I'm the next to die. At the far end of the counter is another man with his hand in a box. He's levitating, and vibrating like a cellphone on silent. He's spraying blood everywhere. I can't stop blinking. I focus on the pawnshop owner.

Between snapshots of light and dark, I see the man's eyes. They burn with fury. I concentrate on them. Part of me welcomes the hate I see in them. I blink, and I see all of us again. Another blink, and I'm back on ground level, standing over John. His eyes are missing.

This is no movie.

There's a sound at the end of the counter and our heads turn to the short man. He isn't vibrating anymore. Like an old photograph, he's still, captured in a moment. We hear the sound again, a crackling, like someone twisting an ice cube tray fresh from the freezer. The noise intensifies. Thin black lines appear over his body. There is a bang, and the short man shatters like glass, crumbling to the floor in thousands of little pieces.

Without a hint of sarcasm, the pawnshop owner says, "It looks like King Amanitore is a pretty good judge of people."

Randy, eyes huge and mouth hanging open, pivots to him.

Gun leveled at the pawnshop owner, he backs up to the glass doors. Reaching them, he yanks on the handle. The door is as frozen as his partner was.

"Unlock these fucking doors!"

The owner doesn't reply. He stands tall, his eyes cold.

Randy rushes to me. His free hand wraps halfway around my neck as he places the barrel of the gun against my temple. Without taking his eyes off of the pawnshop owner, he walks backward, taking me with him to the far end of the counter. We step over pieces of his partner. I can feel him under my sneakers. Randy jabs the barrel twice into the side of my head, forcing my neck to twist to the right.

"Unlock the door now or I swear, I'll kill this kid."

The owner sighs. His eyes dim and his head drops.

I'm ashamed for thinking this, but I want him to unlock the doors. I don't want to die right now. I know there's no way Randy is just going to walk out of here and let us live, but still, I'll be alive that much longer.

The pawnshop owner lifts his head. "I will, but let Billy go."

"Not until you unlock the door."

The owner walks to the counter where he pushed the button earlier. He lifts his hand and holds it over the button. His arm trembles as if he's not sure he can do this. I'm breathing so hard I think I'm going to pass out. *Come on, push the button.* The owner rests his hand on the button for a few seconds, longer than when he pushed it the first time.

*Click.*

Randy continues holding my neck. The pressure increases. "Go to the door and ease it open. If you run out, I'll shoot you first, then the kid."

The owner nods and approaches the door. Reaching it, he pulls it toward him a few inches, then lets go. The door glides shut.

As the pressure on my neck lessens, Randy's arm withdraws completely. I lean against the counter and massage my neck, taking deep breaths. That's when I see something on the counter.

The pawnshop owner walks toward us, taking small,

deliberate steps. "I've unlocked the door and I assume you will now leave us."

Randy chuckles. "No, that's not going to happen."

The pawnshop owner seems unfazed by the response. "I didn't think so. Before you kill us, there's something you should know." He continues his slow pace toward Randy, who doesn't appear to be bothered by it. In fact, he takes a few steps forward of his own with his gun pointed toward the man's waist.

"Oh yeah? And what would that be?"

"I have an associate. His name is Rex. If you kill me, Rex will hunt you down. You won't believe how much you will suffer when Rex finds you. I will also add, we have implements here to insure your agony will be eternal."

"This Rex guy will have to find me first."

"Rex has been around for a long time. He knows how to find people. He will find you."

Randy doesn't reply. His back is to me, so I can't see his face, but the man's words chill me to the bone. I hope they have the same effect on Randy. After seeing what happened to Randy's short partner, I have no doubt the pawnshop owner is telling the truth.

Randy laughs. It's a hardy laugh. I'm stunned. He doesn't believe the owner. I watch him as he raises his arm. The gun is now aimed at the pawnshop owner's chest.

"I'm not scared of you. I'm not scared of this Rex guy. He'll have to get through Mr. Sullivan to find me, and there's no way that'll happen. Say goodbye."

Randy's body stiffens. A second later, he's twisting, falling to the floor. His gun goes off, but I don't flinch. The bullet hits something on one of the shelves against the wall. It breaks and tumbles off the rack. I look down at Randy and notice the large hole in the back of his neck. It's black, and a steady stream of red flows from it. I catch sight of a gun in my hand. It's the short man's gun, the one he put on the counter. For the life of me, I can't remember having reached for it—or using it to kill him. I gaze up at the pawnshop owner. He's staring at me. His neutral expression throws me off guard.

"You did good, Billy."

I nod.

Behind him, the pawnshop's double doors swing open. Standing in the doorway is the biggest man I have ever seen. He's only visible from his chin down. He has to be almost seven feet tall and takes up the width of the doorway. He leans forward and takes two steps inside. My arm is shaking badly, but I manage to raise the gun.

"No, Billy. Don't shoot him," the pawnshop owner says in a calm voice. "That's Rex."

Rex remains standing by the doors. His eyes take in the carnage and, I imagine, looking for threats. After a bit, his gaze settles on the pawnshop owner.

"You're a little late, Rex. We could have used you earlier."

The giant man nods.

An image of Randy suffering in eternal agony comes into my head. It doesn't bother me a bit.

The pawnshop owner shifts to me. "I want to warn you— you are not to mention what has occurred here. You must never mention me, Rex, or the pawnshop. Not to your parents, your friends, or the police."

"How will I explain what happened?"

"That'll be taken care of. I need you to tell Rex and me where you ran into these men."

I tell him everything that happened since I ran into John at the beginning of the trail. He asks me to elaborate on a few things, but other than that, he doesn't interrupt.

When I finish, he stares hard into my eyes. "Billy, never walk into this pawnshop again."

Any sense of bonding I had with the man vanishes. I find myself taking a step back from him. He closes the distance and touches my forehead. My eyes close.

I hear men talking and radio chatter. I open my eyes. There's a young woman in a white uniform peering down at me; I see the tops of trees and the sky behind her. She's all excited about our eye contact, and calls out to someone that I am conscious. *Where the heck am I?* I sit up, forcing her to pull back. Craning my head, I try to figure out what's going on.

There are police all around me, walking back and forth, searching the ground for something. I recognize the area. *I'm at Glen Lake.* Looking past them and to the left, I see a white sheet lying over something on the ground. *That's where the two men shot Mr. Day.* In the opposite direction is Devil's Rock. There are more police there. And there's another white sheet on the ground. Someone taps the back of my shoulder and I look over. It's a policeman.

"Hey, son. I need to ask you some questions. Are you up to it?"

Gazing around, I see that everyone has stopped in their tracks, looking at me. I nod.

"Good. First, I need to know if it was only you and your fishing buddy involved with this man and the teacher."

*Fishing buddy?*

*John!*

My stomach churns when I remember what happened to him.

*This man?*

I'm about to tell him that there were two men, then the warning from the pawnshop owner comes back to me.

"Yes," I reply.

The policeman sighs. "Okay. One more question. Did you or your fishing buddy have a gun with you?"

I'm not sure why he's asking me this, but I make the mistake of looking at my hand before I answer.

"No."

He stares at me. He knows I'm hiding something. "One last question before we take you to the hospital. Do you know who would have called to tell us you were out here?"

I shake my head. Meeting his gaze "No. I don't."

He won't look away from me. It's a contest I know he can't win. Finally, he understands this, too.

"All right," he says. "We'll talk again later."

It's been three weeks since John was killed. I've since learned they found the bodies of John and Randy on the ground by

Devil's Rock, and the body of Mr. Day in the lake that after-noon. They also found two guns at the scene, one of which had my prints on it. That gun was used to shoot Randy in the neck. I told them I had no memory of the event from the time John and I made it to Devil's Rock until I woke up with the emergency people around me. The detective in charge of the case didn't believe me. He said there was another set of fingerprints on the gun, that there *had* to have been another person at the scene. I continued to tell the detective I couldn't remember. He made me go back to Devil's Rock with him. He said it was to spur my memory. We took the same route John and I had when we ran away from the two men. I took note that the building on Church Street was still there, but the pawnshop was gone.

Word spread quickly that I was a hero. I had killed the man who had murdered John and Mr. Day. I told my parents, the kids at school, and the newspapers the same story—that I didn't remember anything from the moment we arrived at Devil's Rock. It didn't matter though; everyone treats me differently now. Everyone wants to be my friend and my old pals want to hang around me more. Heck, even Vivian is willing to let me go further with her.

The thing is, I'm different, too, now.

When I'm outside walking around, sometimes I see a shadow. I catch it out of the corner of my eye, and when I turn, it takes on the appearance of a huge man. The shadow man stares at me until I look away. It's never there when I look again. I've also seen the pawnshop. It's now in the bottom of a three-decker in the center of town, next to the bridge. It has those same tinted windows so I can't see inside. Any temptation I have to go into the pawnshop and speak with the owner is dashed when I think of the shadow man.

Rex.

I do my best to avoid that area.

# STORY NOTES (STANLEY'S HOLE)

*I*wanted to write a story in the vein of Jeff Strand—dark-humored horror, heavy on dialog. After finishing "Stanley's Hole", I submitted the tale to my writers' group and awaited their reactions. Before the meeting started, a few of the members shook their heads and laughed. It went over well, so I thought I would submit it to any anthology call I came upon.

I sent it to two anthologies and was rejected by both. I knew it was an odd story so I wasn't as upset as I normally get when an email arrives telling me I've failed miserably and I should give up any notion of being a writer.

They say good things come in threes, and the third time I submitted it was the charm. Dark Eclipse bought the story, and the editor sent me a nice note saying how much she enjoyed the story.

I ran into Jeff Strand shortly after the sale and I commenced to tell him how I sold a story that was inspired by his style of writing. He seemed genuinely pleased, and that meant almost as much to me than the sale itself.

# STANLEY'S HOLE

Stanley sat up in a panic, his eyes as large as hard-boiled eggs. His arms thrashed at things out of reach, and he exhaled so heavily his breath could have put out a small fire. Not quite awake yet, he couldn't beat back the horrific images from his nightmare.

Stanley felt his stomach begin to roil. Rolling to his right, he vomited four times onto the floor before he was reduced to dry heaving. With a string of milky drool hanging from his lips, he pulled back and rested his head on the pillow. Wide awake now, he wiped the dregs from his mouth onto his pajama sleeve.

"Stanley," his wife said to him as she turned on her night-stand lamp, "what's wrong? Are you sick?"

He sighed. Then, looking over his slime-covered arm, he replied in a croaky voice, "No. Well, just a little. I had a night-mare. I can't remember ever having one that was so vivid and disgusting."

"Oh, honey. Maybe you shouldn't stay up so late reading those horror novels."

With a grimace he turned to her. He was going to argue that the horror novel had nothing to do with the nightmare but decided it wasn't worth the effort. Besides, the book wasn't all that scary. No, the nightmare was worse than any novel he had read or any movie he had ever seen.

"I'll clean this up in a minute," he replied trying to avoid any more discussion of the nightmare. "Then I'll head into work a little early."

"Can you clean it up now? It smells really bad."

Stanley's drive to work was usually short and uneventful, but this morning it felt like the longest ten minutes of his life. He couldn't get that damn nightmare out of his head. Several times he felt his hands tighten on the steering wheel to the point of turning white, and twice he found himself shivering despite the heat of the morning. Thankfully, it was the end of the month. He knew he would be preoccupied all day with shipping and loading trucks so the company could meet its sales quota. He should be busy enough to forget about the nightmare.

When he pulled into the company's parking lot, Stanley had never been more grateful to see the drab, concrete walls of the factory. Since he had arrived early, there was an open parking spot close to the employee entrance. He glided into the space, turned his car off, grabbed his lunch bucket, and walked to the door. He barely made it to the corner of the building before stopping dead in his tracks.

There was a hole, no bigger than a quarter, on the side of the building. It struck Stanley that it was darker than any hole he had ever seen, despite the thin, wispy curls of pale smoke floating from it. A cold fist gripped his spine; he'd never seen a hole that disturbed him as much as this one.

He took that thought back. He had seen a hole as disturbing as this one. It was in his nightmare last night. Stanley's mouth opened wide at the memory, and his lunch bucket fell from his hand. Unable to take his eyes away from the hole, he trembled.

He forced himself to close his eyes tightly, to chase away both the sight of the hole and his overwhelming fear. When he reopened his eyes seconds later, a gasp escaped from his mouth. The smoke was now thicker, darker, and it billowed steadily from the hole. If this had anything to do with his nightmare, Stanley thought he knew what was about to happen. He hadn't a clue how to stop it. In desperation, he did the only thing that he could think to do—he rushed to the hole and stuck his forefinger into it.

His shoulders tensed in anticipation. He waited for his finger to be lopped off or burned black to the bone.

Seconds passed.

Nothing happened.

His shoulders relaxed.

Stanley looked over his situation and thanked God that the hole was chest high. At least he felt no discomfort from stooping or reaching.

He studied his arm and wondered how long he could stand in place before he grew too tired to keep his finger in the hole. Out of the recesses of his memory, he recalled something from his nightmare. He worriedly glanced at his watch. It blinked 6:55 a.m. In his dream, the shit hit the fan at 6:55 a.m. and that it was all over by 7:10 a.m.

He had to keep his finger in the hole for fifteen minutes— only fifteen minutes! *Well, that's doable,* he thought with some relief. He concentrated on the watch.

"Hey, Stanley! Stanley! What the fuck ya doing?"

Stanley turned to see his co-worker, Brian, making his way to the employee entrance. When Stanley didn't reply, Brian continued with his line of questioning.

"Shit, man, what's up? Why are ya stickin' yer finger into the wall?"

Stanley sighed. "I'm trying to save the world, Brian. Now, please, leave me alone."

Brian's eyes went to Stanley's hand, then to his face, and back to his hand. Brian looked confused, but concern was evident in his voice when he stepped closer to Stanley and asked, "You think somethin's gonna come out of that hole and you can stop it by stickin' a finger in it or somethin', Stanley?"

Turning his back to Brian, Stanley sighed again. "Yes, Brian, that's exactly what I think. Now please, go away."

"But Stan, our shift starts in five minutes. Yer gonna be late! Hogwalls is gonna be pissed if yer late!"

Stanley hadn't thought about that. Hogwalls didn't take too well to his employees being late for work. He turned again to Brian to ask him if he could tell Hogwalls that he'd be along in a few minutes and saw that Brian had company. There were four or five other employees standing behind Brian, gawking at Stanley, and there were more headed his way from the parking lot.

"Hey, Stanley, what the heck are you doing?" asked Fred.

"Stanley, why's your finger in the wall?" Pete said.

"Stanley, that's not a pussy you know!" Hank laughed.

On and on it went. Stanley's face grew red with embarrassment and he looked down at his shoes. Still, no matter what they said or how much fun they made of him, he vowed that he wouldn't pull his finger from the hole. However, when he heard the next voice, years of training kicked in, and he looked up again.

"What the hell you guys doing out here? Come on, it's seven o'clock; get to work!" It was Hogwalls.

Laughing and jeering, the men left to go punch in—except for Hogwalls, who approached Stanley.

"What are you doing, Stanley?" he asked gruffly.

"I'm saving the world, boss."

"How's that, Stanley?"

Stanley explained the nightmare he had—how, when he was walking into the building, he saw the same hole in the wall that he had seen in his dream.

Hogwalls silently studied Stanley for a moment. Stanley knew he was a good worker, not prone to making excuses when he messed up and he was not a joking kind of guy. He hoped that Hogwalls felt the same way.

Hogwalls sighed. Softening his tone, he asked him, "Stanley, exactly what was it you saw in your nightmare?"

Stanley gulped. He was reluctant to provide the details, but he realized that if he didn't explain himself, he could be fired.

"It was bad, Boss. Something evil floated out of this hole. So evil that it eventually destroyed the whole world. I know this hole looks small, and it was small in my dream, too, but there was something damned big behind it. It caused snakes to swallow little boys. It made mothers eat their babies. I saw men who worked in a nuclear power plant dumping waste into drinking water supplies. I watched as workers in a sausage factory put pieces of glass into meat. Surgeons were nicking arteries on purpose and then sewing patients back up. Men were having sex with dogs, and the dogs liked it."

The expression on his boss's face remained neutral as Stanley recounted his nightmare, but by the end, Hogwalls stare turned hard, giving Stanley hope that he was getting through to him.

Stanley concluded, "It was like there were waves of evil sweeping across the world, and it all came from this hole."

Hogwalls, his hands shaking slightly and his eyes darting back and forth between Stanley and the hole, took a few moments to digest his employee's story. Eventually his eyes locked on Stanley.

"Look, Stanley," he said, "it's seven-oh-five. How much longer do you have to plug up that hole?"

"Just five more minutes, Boss. Just give me five more minutes, then, I can...Ahhh!"

"Stanley, what's the matter?"

"Something's got my finger, Boss! Ahhh. It hurts!"

Hogwalls rushed to the wall and placed his hands on Stanley's arm.

"No!" Stanley cried, "You can't take my finger from the hole! Please, no! Boss, leave it there, I'm begging you!"

Hogwalls stared at Stanley for a moment and then looked back at the wall. He shook his head and started to address Stanley, "You're crazy, Stanley! There's nothing..." He stopped speaking in mid-sentence, then turned rigid noticing a small stream of blood mixed with slivers of bone flowing out from the space between Stanley's finger and the hole. He looked at Stanley with terror in his eyes, jumped back, and shouted, "My God! There *IS* something in there!"

"Ahhh! I told you there was! Boss, how much longer do I have?"

Hogwalls looked at his watch and screamed out the answer, "You've got two more minutes, Stanley! You've got to hang on for two more minutes!"

If Stanley had thought his ride to work this morning was the longest ten minutes of his life, it was nothing compared to the next two.

Behind the wall, something chewed on Stanley's finger. The pressure from the bites was severe, like a vise, continuingly tightening and loosening. His bones were pulverized with every crushing chomp and his nerve endings were aflame.

Twice he thought he would pass out, but both times, he managed to hang on.

"How much longer, Boss?" Stanley asked between gritted teeth.

Hogwalls was shaking so hard he had to use his free arm to steady his watch hand. Sweat dripped down from his forehead as he replied in a loud voice, "Ten seconds, Stanley. Hang on!" He paused and then began a countdown. "Eight seconds, seven, six, five, four, three, two, one! It's seven-ten, Stanley! You can pull your finger out now! Do it now!"

Despite the agony, Stanley waited a few more seconds before removing his finger from the wall. He had to be sure that all of his suffering wasn't in vain because of a timepiece that was off by a few seconds.

Satisfied that he had waited long enough, he pulled his hand back. Though he knew what to expect, the sight caused him to scream.

His finger had been chewed off to the second knuckle. Blood poured from the stump. Stanley could see bone and gristle gleaming white at the joint. Terrified, he waved his hand in the air and turned to Hogwalls.

Blood hit Hogwalls in the face, but instead of moving out of the way, his boss stood motionless, in shock.

Tasting Stanley's blood jolted Hogwalls to his senses. He grabbed Stanley's arm and held it tight. "Let's get you inside." Hogwalls' voice was low, reassuring. "We need to stop the blood flow and then get you to a hospital."

Led inside the building, Stanley made an effort to calm down and speak to his boss. He looked at Hogwalls, staring straight into his eyes, and asked, "I did it, Boss, didn't I?"

Hogwalls returned the stare, and then, with a smile that betrayed little emotion, he answered Stanley. "Yes, Stanley, you did it."

Both men turned a corner, heading to the first-aid station nearby. Neither of them could see the packs of dogs lining up, single file, outside in the parking lot.

# STORY NOTES (THE LITTLE MAN)

*T*hese next two tales are the first completed stories I wrote. Published in a writer's thread in Nanci Kalanta's Horror World website, I rediscovered them while going through my computer in preparation for this collection. I debated whether to include them, but after rereading the stories, I decided to add them.

The old Horror World message board had members who aspired to be writers. We were voracious readers and would discuss the genre endlessly. Many prominent horror authors visited the site and shared their publishing experiences and writing processes with us. Encouragement from these authors was abundant, so a group of us decided to try our hand at writing a short story.

We decided to treat our attempts as an exercise. Those who were interested would write a story of around 1,500 words and submit it to a moderator who would post the work without the author's name attached. This way, we could offer feedback on the stories without prejudice, and the author could read the comments without public embarrassment. To up the ante, we asked established authors to read the stories and provide their feedback. To our delight, all of the authors we contacted agreed to participate. Steve Vernon, Tom Picirrilli, Robert Dunbar, Gary Braunbeck, and others served as guest experts to critique our work.

The moderators chose the theme of the story, then we would have one month to write it. Some excellent stories were written during these exercises. Tales by Keith Minnion and Thad Linson eventually made their way into paying markets.

In one of these exercises, the moderator asked us to write a story *paying tribute to Richard Laymon, an author we had discussed often on the message board. Laymon's prose is known for its over-the-top violence, expressive dialog, and some of the most imaginative sexual narratives in horror. Using as many of his tropes as I could in a very short story, I wrote "The Little Man".*

# THE LITTLE MAN

Melanie was conscious.

It was strange, but her first thought was wondering if someone had hit the *on* switch in her brain, commanding her synapses to fire. The only problem was who, or whatever it was that jolted her awake, had forgotten to turn on another switch—the one for the lights.

Blinking furiously, Melanie tried to chase away the darkness and concentrate, but the results were poor at best. All she could do was distinguish contrasting shades of black in the shadows. It was disorienting. With no way to determine up or down, she had trouble figuring out if she was lying or sitting up.

Thinking a change of direction might put things into perspective, Melanie moved her head to the left. At least, she attempted to, but nothing happened. Confused, she tried to move it in the other direction. Once again, nothing happened. Worry crept into her thoughts so she began to experiment. She rolled her eyes, puffed her cheeks, snorted out her nose, and then ran her tongue over her teeth. Everything seemed to be in working order so she breathed a small sigh of relief. It was short lived. Her worry turned to panic when it came time to move her arms.

Not only wouldn't her arms respond to her thoughts, neither would her legs. Like an oncoming truck, fear slammed into her when she realized that she couldn't feel anything below her neck. Was she paralyzed? One thing for certain, she wasn't deaf. She could plainly hear her own loud sobbing escaping from her lips.

"Melanie? Is that you?"

"Yes, yes, it's me! Please help me! I can't move!"

"Melanie, it's me, Rob. I can't move either, but I can hear you. You sound like you're above me somewhere. Can you see anything?"

"No, everything's dark. You sound like you're close though, Rob, right below me. What happened? Where are we?"

"I—I don't know. The last thing I remember is being with you down by the lake."

Memories rushed into Melanie's head. She and Rob were lying on a blanket and going at it heavy. He already had her shirt unbuttoned and her bra unclasped. She remembered his hands being warm and gentle, her nipples responding quickly. She recalled closing her eyes after he lowered his lips to her breasts and began sucking, but then she recalled hearing a noise, a shuffling behind Rob. Opening her eyes at the sound, she saw him—a little man wearing a ski mask. Both of his hands held something high. She pulled away from Rob, trying to disengage her breast from his mouth, but his lips followed along with her.

More images flashed in her mind: one of the little man's hands coming down and plunging something into Rob's neck; Rob going limp and falling away, her breasts jostling as she tried to crawl from him; then, the little man's other hand coming down quickly to her own neck.

"I remember what happened, Rob!"

"What—what happened to us?"

"Some man, a little guy, he attacked us! He stuck us with a needle and that's the last I remember!"

"Fuck! Maybe that's why we can't move—he stuck us with something that paralyzed us."

"Rob, do you think he buried us alive?"

"I don't think so. I can feel my face, and there's nothing on or around it."

"Then where the hell are we?"

Before Rob could answer, Melanie screamed.

Her eyes burned as light exploded in front of her. Shutting them immediately, she reflexively tried to turn to the side, but her head still refused to move. And, though she hadn't seen the source of the light, she had an idea as to what it might be. The sounds of squeaky hinges filled her ears. After a few moments, she opened her eyes, being careful to acclimate herself to the light.

Melanie saw that she was in a small room, mostly empty with the exception of a bed with its headboard pressed firmly against a wall in front of her. The figure of a little man in the doorway, one hand on a light switch and the body of a girl draped over his shoulder, slipped into her view. The girl was struggling, but not with much effort. Melanie wondered if he had drugged her as he did them.

Without a word, the man turned off the light, and with only the illumination from the open door, Melanie watched as he tossed the girl onto the bed. He removed the girl's clothing and tossed the articles onto the floor. When she was naked, he shook off his own clothes and then mounted the girl.

"Hey, what the fuck are you doing?" It was Rob's voice shouting somewhere below her.

The little man ignored Rob and began to pump harder into the girl, who continued to lightly struggle.

"Hey, asshole, leave her the fuck alone! Is that the only way you can have sex with a girl? By drugging her? Is that the only way you can be a big man?"

The man stopped in mid-thrust and turned to stare in Melanie's and Rob's direction. He rolled off the girl, bent down, picked something off the floor, and menancingly walked toward them.

Melanie heard Rob begin to speak again, but before he could utter a full word, his voice was muffled. She heard a gagging sound, and Rob went quiet.

"Enjoy the flavor, Rob," the little man said sadistically. "That's the only way you're ever going to taste pussy again."

Melanie shouted, "What have you done to Rob? And leave that poor girl alone!"

The man walked back toward the door and flipped the light switch. Melanie's eyes were blinded again, but not as badly as before. When her eyes adjusted to the light, she gazed at the man and gasped. "Dr. Snyder?"

Standing before her was their college biology teacher.

"Yes, Melanie, it's me."

"But—but why?"

"I've been working on an experiment for the past ten years, and I think I've finally found the right combinations of chemicals to make it a success."

"I—I don't understand. What does that have to do with Rob and me?"

"Let me show you, Melanie." Dr. Snyder walked outside Melanie's line of vision for a moment, and returned holding something large in his hands. "I want you to look into this, Melanie, and tell me what you see." Dr. Snyder then raised the object in his hands.

Melanie was confused. She was looking at a picture of her face. No, not a picture, but a reflection. He was holding up a mirror to her. "I still don't understand," she replied nervously. Dr. Snyder started to step away from her, but when he had only moved back a few feet, Melanie screamed once more.

In the mirror, Melanie saw a bookcase. On the top shelf of the bookcase was her head. Just her head. As Dr. Snyder took a few more steps backward, Rob's head came into view on a shelf below hers, a pair of panties stuffed into his mouth.

Dr. Snyder laughed, "After all those years of research... well... let's just say my resurrection dreams have been realized, Melanie. If you're wondering where the remainder of your bodies are, well... since I had no use for Rob's, I dismembered it and buried it in the woods. As for yours..."

Melanie's mind began to freeze, her thoughts draining away. She embraced the oncoming void, and Dr. Snyder's voice faded as he continued speaking.

"I admit to always having a crush on you, Melanie. I wanted you since the moment I first saw you in my class, but I knew I couldn't have you. At least, as you were. Look, that's you on the bed, Melanie, just lying there waiting with your legs spread open. Now, if you'll excuse me, I'd like to finish what I started. Oh, by the way, are you using any birth control?"

# STORY NOTES (BURNING RAIN)

*I*f *you've read this collection from front to back, "Burning Rain" will seem familiar. It's because "Burning Rain" is the short story from which* Steel *was born". If you've saved* Steel *for last, reading "Burning Rain" will not act as a spoiler.*

*"Burning Rain" is another product of the Horror World exercise threads. It's a horror tale with elements of fantasy and science fiction, two genres in which I was not well-versed. At the time, I was reading quite a bit of Gary Braunbeck's fiction, and his influence is apparent in the story.*

*After posting "Burning Rain" at Horror World, the feedback, as I remember, was tepid. Initially, there were no raves, the comments were not memorable. Feeling a bit down, I considered the story a failed exercise.*

*Then, Kurt Criscione happened. Kurt, a member of the message board, loved the story. He wrote how he enjoyed the premise, the characters, and the word play. His review stayed with me.*

*Much later, I started a novella entitled* The Strange Saga of Mattie Dyer *I contemplated expanding it into a novel, and recalling Kurt's review, I decided to incorporate "Burning Rain" into the work.* Steel *was to be the middle portion of a themed trilogy of novellas, all revolving around a mysterious hole. Though I haven't completed the trilogy, it's never far from my mind.*

# BURNING RAIN

Chalk stood before me, shoulders slumped as he stared at my blistered hand. Though drool wasn't spilling out between his lips, he looked like an idiot with his mouth open and his eyes bulged out. When he had had enough of gawking at my hand, he raised his head and made eye contact with me. Worry lines creased his brow. In the moment, I parceled a measure of pity for him. I shrugged—our usual sign to let him know I was all right. Chalk averted his eyes, nodded, and slipped into a corner of the shelter, dragging his guilt along with him. Let him. What was I thinking? The little prick deserved to suffer. It was the second time this month I saved his ass because he got back too late.

What I had really wanted to do was to shove my hand right into that mouth of his and let him choke on it for what he did to me. Fuck his concern. Because of him, *I'm* in pain, and it hurts like hell. My hand is bright pink from the rain and the skin had peeled back some. Thankfully, the burn didn't go all that deep, which was a small relief. The last thing I could afford to be doing is changing bloody dressings for the next week or two.

Hell, maybe I'm a little too hard on him. I guess every one of us here has fucked up one time or another. But you know, it should make us learn to be more careful when we screw up. Instead, we all seem to be getting more careless, or *more dumber* as Sherlock says. He's one to talk though. It's Sherlock's fault that Rose is gone. It wasn't the burning rain that got Rose; it was the spidler and, damn, there was no excuse for it. Sherlock was in charge of her. It was him who was supposed to make sure Rose came back from the park an hour before closing, but he let her play outside too long. Shit, she was just a little kid, she didn't know no better. Sherlock's got to live with it though, however long that will be. He pretends like it's just one more of us dying, but you can tell it's messed him up, watching that spidler eat Rose up whole like that. Spidlers like to take their time eating, too. I wonder how long Sherlock listened to Rose's screams before he couldn't take it anymore and left her there.

It's too bad about Rose. What a waste. There' are only five of us left. Why only five? Well, the others are gone because those stupid bastards were careless, too.

Maybe Sherlock's right. Maybe we are getting *more dumber.*

An adult grabbed Sneakers two days ago when he reached for a can while foraging in a grocery store. Sneakers is the one kid who should have known better. Shit, he'd been a food hunter a lot longer than any of us were. He knew there was no more canned food for the taking, at least none in plain sight. It was a stupid trap, one that you could see from a mile away, but hell, maybe Sneakers was so hungry he wasn't thinking. Okay, maybe he was thinking and he just didn't give a shit. Being dead can't be any worse than the way things are now. The thing is, we don't really know if Sneakers is dead, as he might still be alive. That poor bastard. If he is alive, I bet he wishes he wasn't. Adults will fuck you up good, worse than the rain.

Speaking of the rain, Crayon, well, she got all burned up last week. It was odd, because she knew it was getting dark and the burning rain was coming. She just sat on that old chair in front of the shelter ignoring us and reading one of the salvaged books. I still wonder if she didn't hear us calling for her to come in, or if it was her plan to stay outside as late as she did. From the window, we all watched her die. That wasn't the worst part. The worst part is that we had to scrape her up the next morning. Nobody wants to walk past that shit every day. The whole thing was a shame really. We could have used her tonight.

I can't forget Jersey. He was tough, but not tough enough, I guess. A gorildog tore him to pieces last month, but not before he managed to tear one of the damn thing's limbs off. The gorildog wolfed him down right there on the spot. After it finished with him, the damned thing ate its own fucking limb.

And so it goes...

I shouldn't think about this shit. It's depressing. Bad enough we have to spend our evenings in this hellhole. I know, I don't have to make it worse thinking about the guys that are gone, but I can't stop. Especially Wise.

Wise was the one guy that kept everything from falling apart here. He gave us all our assignments. He told us what to look for when we were foraging. He gave us weapons. He taught us how to read the few books we had.

He called those books *folk tales*, but I think they are more than that. I liked *To Kill a Mockingbird* and *Catcher in the Rye*, but it's hard to believe in a world like the ones in those books. Shit, who the hell ever thought up a book where adults weren't killing and eating kids? Who'd ever believe there were girls like Scout and boys like Holden? Let me tell you, those two wouldn't last a minute in the real world. My favorite book was *The Day the Towers Fell*. At least that seems true to life. Wise never liked reading it though. After I would ask him to read from it, for some reason, he would get real quiet. If he picked me to sleep with him that night, well, instead of sex, he'd hug me tight until I fell asleep.

I loved Wise. I know he loved me.

Yeah, someone might take that to mean we had an awful lot of sex. They'd be right. Though I was his favorite, Wise had sex with all the girls. Only Jersey thought that it was wrong, that we should pick partners and stick with them. Well, Jersey's not here anymore, is he? Then again, neither is Wise. I shouldn't even give a shit, should stop thinking about both of them. But I can't. It might help if I knew which one of them knocked me up. But then again, it might not. After the baby is born and it's time to feed, well, I don't really want to know which of them is the daddy of my breakfast.

It's almost time to sleep. It's getting dark, and we have to be quiet. Especially late at night. That's when the boomers come. Yes, even while the burning rain falls. Any noise, loud or soft, will cause them to come at you. No matter how many times they've tried to crash their way in and failed, it stills scares me. Wise had put steel up over the windows a long time ago, and we really beefed up the doors, but still, you don't want 'em booming against the building. I just hope they don't find the cracks on the back wall.

I've got to pick one of us tonight.

I don't want to do it, but hell, it's been too damn long. I wish Chalk had the balls that Wise had. Wise knew what he had to do to keep us alive. Okay, maybe it was guilt that caused Wise to make his decision. Who knows? Though he never admitted it, I could tell he knew what happened to make this world all fucked up. Maybe he was part of the reason. He always told me it didn't used to be like this, but if that's true, he's the only one of us who knows why.

I remember that night he gathered us around him, telling us what he was going to do and why. Not that he had to, we all knew. I can still see him there, in the middle of the room, stripped naked and picking up a piece of glass. He didn't say a word when he plunged it into his belly. I don't think he knew how painful it would be because when he tried to open himself up more, he fell down onto his back moaning, really loud, too. When he figured out he couldn't finish it, he looked over at me and nodded. I knew what I had to do. Grabbing some gloves, I took hold of the glass, and ripped open his belly. I continued up his chest as far as I could go. Sitting him up against the back wall, I used both my hands to widen the cut enough to let his intestines fall out. I remember them steaming in the cool air. We all made a mass rush for the food. Yeah, it was raw and bloody, but we were so hungry none of us cared. We ate good that night. Nothing went to waste.

And now, I gotta pick someone to feed us. I think I've made my decision. It's time to find out what kind of balls Chalk really has.

# ABOUT THE AUTHOR

Tony Tremblay is the author of the Bram Stoker nominated novel *The Moore House*, and the short story collection *The Seeds of Nightmares*. Tremblay has worked as a reviewer of horror and genre novels for *Horror World, Cemetery Dance Magazine,* and *Beware The Dark Magazine*. The author has also hosted a television show called The Taco Society Presents which showcased New England horror and genre writers and artists. He will host another television show in the fall of 2019 featuring classic horror movies. Tremblay lives in Goffstown, New Hampshire, along with his wife Paula.

Curious about other Crossroad Press books?
Stop by our site:
http://store.crossroadpress.com
We offer quality writing
in digital, audio, and print formats.

Enter the code FIRSTBOOK
to get 20% off your first order from our store!
Stop by today!

47636942R00119

Made in the USA
Middletown, DE
10 June 2019